Kevin Hearne

Kevin Hearne

This special signed edition
is limited to 1250 numbered
copies and 26 lettered copies.

This is copy __1065__ .

A QUESTION OF NAVIGATION

A QUESTION OF NAVIGATION

KEVIN HEARNE

SUBTERRANEAN PRESS
2021

DAY 2: LABOR DAY, SEPTEMBER 5, 2022

They abducted me yesterday and I'm not sure how accurate my timekeeping will be after this. Ship days are going to be different than Earth days—they don't even use the same units of measurement that we do, much less have a planet that turns on its axis once in the equivalent of twenty-four hours. Plus, time dilation is going to kick in as we approach the speed of light, so I suppose it won't matter what day of the week I think it is after this. I can worry about the date if I ever get back to Earth.

A list of my more immediate worries includes:
• Probes, and
• Uh, that's it really. Just probes

I mean Emily promised they wouldn't eat me, so that pretty much leaves
• Probes

Especially since I brought up the subject with Emily and she gave me a very telling series of non-answers to my very clear and direct questions.

ME: Are you guys going to probe me?

EMILY: Silly! Why would you even ask that?

ME: Alien abductions are practically a whole genre of fiction with us, and in those stories the aliens always conduct exploratory probes on the humans even when they lack a logical reason to do so. There's a squelching sound and then a lot of screaming and we have nightmares about it. I think it's safe to say that as a species we have a primal fear of being probed by other sentient life forms. It's second only, in fact, to being eaten by other life forms, and you already promised you wouldn't eat me.

EMILY: Yes, we've decided to keep you alive, and aren't you happy about that? We got you these nice clothes that say DO NOT EAT all over them in our language.

ME: I'm really happy about that. Seriously, thank you. I even like the clothes. But can you also promise right now not to probe me?

EMILY: I don't even know what probing really is and I'm a little worried that we're not doing right by you. You said it's a squelching noise?

ME: Hold on, now. Don't pretend you don't know what probing is. I know that you speak my language fluently, so I just want to hear you say you won't probe me.

EMILY: Hmm, you know what, Clint? This sounds really important and I don't want to mess it up because I missed some nuance here, so let me get back to you on this.

ME: What? Wait, no. Emily, there is *nothing* nuanced about a probe!

EMILY: I'll circle back later.

They are going to fucking probe me.

I can't use my phone to take any notes because they took it, and in any case it's dead and the ship doesn't have a charger or compatible power sources. But Emily gave me a stack of notebooks they stole from somewhere along with some pens and told me to write whatever I wanted. No expectation of privacy, so, you know. Hi Emily, or whichever of you is reading this. Thanks for not eating me. I really appreciate it.

But I want to write down how I got here before my calendar fills up with probes and my memory goes because they removed it.

Derek and I were enjoying a post-pandemic hike in Rocky Mountain National Park on the Bierstadt trail when we came upon two girls who looked to be under ten years old. They were unaccompanied by adults. There was nobody coming up the trail behind them, and no one behind us.

One of them was a white girl wearing a t-shirt with a pink unicorn on it. She had a matching baseball cap on over a mane of blond hair and a pair of pink jeans. The second girl wasn't white and she had a black Colorado Rockies baseball cap over her straight dark hair. There was something off about both of them— their eyes were a bit too big.

"Here's two," the unicorn girl said, gesturing at us. "Can I have one of them?"

"Maybe," her companion said, looking at the trail behind us and then quickly glancing back over her shoulder before addressing us. "Hello, misters."

"Hello," we replied, and I asked, "Are your parents around?"

The unicorn girl looked at her buddy. "Why is he asking about our parents?"

"I've run into this before. We look like children to them and it triggers paternalistic instincts."

Unicorn girl blinked. "Well, that was a fairly egregious miscalculation."

"No, it's actually fortuitous. We don't register as a threat to them so they're not even behaving cautiously, much less exhibiting a fight-or-flight response. See? They're just standing there looking dumb."

The first girl swung her gaze back to us to verify that statement. "Hmm. You appear to be correct."

Hearing children talk like that instantly creeped me out and I tugged at Derek's sleeve to back off, but he either missed the bad vibe or didn't care and he asked, "Are you lost? Where are you supposed to be?"

"Right here," unicorn girl said. "It's time for me to feed. Which one, Emily? Is it possible to determine by sight which would be more delicious?"

"Maintain control and be patient," Emily said, a tiny scowl of disapproval on her features. But then she turned to us and flashed what was meant to be a charming, reassuring smile, except that it looked like there might have been more than a single row of teeth in her mouth. "Gentlemen. Do either of you possess an advanced degree from a university?"

"We both do," Derek said. "Are you okay? What happened to your teeth?"

Emily ignored his question and asked another. "What degrees do you possess?"

"English," Derek said.

Emily's too-large eyes narrowed and the smile disappeared. "I see. And you, mister?"

"Physics," I said. Her toothy grin immediately returned.

"Ah! Physics! No doubt you are struggling with embarrassing gaps in your knowledge, but we can work with that."

She turned to the unicorn girl and waved a hand dismissively at Derek. "You can eat the English major, Janelle."

"Hey, what?" Derek said.

"Yes! Finally!" Janelle took off her hat and her hair came with it. The whole thing had been a wig, and underneath was

OH SHIT—

DAY 3, SEPT 6, I THINK: THEY LIE

Emily interrupted me yesterday in the worst possible way. She entered the little room they had assigned me as I was writing and smiled that sharp-toothed smile she thought was winsome and innocent but gave me the shuddering heaves.

"Clint, how about if we promise there won't be any squelching and therefore no reason to scream? We'll be very gentle. Would that be okay?"

"No! It would not be okay! I don't want to be probed!"

"But you led me to believe that squelching was a key component of the horror for you. Was that incorrect?"

"No, but it's incorrect to think that squelching or lack thereof is a negotiating point. It's not the methodology of the probing that creates our visceral horror, it's the probing itself. It's the violation."

"We don't intend to violate you in any way. We're just going to talk to you and monitor your brain activity."

"Passive monitoring? Nothing being done to my brain?"

"Nothing at all. It's like an electroencephalograph. You're familiar with those?"

"Yes."

"Great! So there's nothing to worry about."

"Well, you've abducted me and I'm on a ship full of aliens that have to be told not to eat me on sight, so I find that pretty worrisome."

"Oh, Clint. You're so silly. Let me assure you that you're perfectly safe," she said.

"What if I say no?"

"Then I will be forced to change your designation to food."

"Are you serious?"

"I'm just kidding! Ha ha. But don't say no, okay?" There really were rows of teeth when she smiled. I gulped down a cold lump of fear.

"Okay."

"Thanks. Come with me."

She led me out the door and took a sharp left down a dark gray hallway made of the same unfamiliar but ubiquitous composite material in my quarters. Everything looked like extruded slabs, and though it must have been intended for aliens, it wasn't that different from what human quarters would look like.

A few turns and we ended up in a room with several people in white lab coats and baseball caps. They appeared to be human adults at first glance, but they all had those too-big eyes and too-sharp teeth. There was a chair similar to the kind one sees in the dentist's office and a lot of equipment that looked designed for medical purposes.

"Please take off your clothes," Emily said.

"My clothes? Why is that necessary? You said it was just brain monitoring."

"It'll make things easier if we require further tests. Take them off."

"But I like them. Especially how they say DO NOT EAT all over."

"Well, we can put you at ease right now. Everyone, this is Clint. I need each of you to give him your solemn vow that you will not eat him so that we can proceed in a spirit of cooperation."

An alien who looked like a Latina woman said her name was Maria and she promised not to eat me.

Another who seemed to be Black like me said his name was Antoine and he wouldn't be hungry for days.

The third appeared to be of Arabic descent. He introduced himself as Ahmed and vowed not to eat me. But I knew that regardless of how utterly normal they appeared, they were hiding something underneath those ballcaps and they ate people.

"Great work, everybody!" Emily said. "Clint, get naked."

I didn't think for one second I was safe, but I figured that proceeding was marginally safer than refusing and getting reassigned as food. I disrobed and sat down in the chair. Maria and Ahmed began attaching sensors to my head, while Antoine hung back with Emily, the two of them consulting handheld tablets in their hands. They weren't rubbing their hands together in evil glee, so maybe it was going to be okay after all.

"Mind if I ask you a question, Maria? Or Ahmed?" I said.

"Sure," Ahmed replied, taping a sensor to my temple. "Go ahead."

"We're heading back to your home world, right? We're underway right now?"

"That's right."

"There's gravity on board that feels pretty normal, so either you're generating that somehow or we're accelerating constantly at one gee."

"Right. The second one. Or close to it. Our planet is .98 of your gravity, so just marginally slower than your one gee."

"Okay, so why are you still in your human forms? Why bother maintaining the illusion?"

Maria answered that one. "For your comfort. We've found that our natural shape stimulates a fear response in humans that's counterproductive. Look at how cooperative you're being. It's really best for all of us."

Ahmed snorted. "That's the truth. Imagine how insane they'd be down in Food Storage if we weren't—"

Emily interrupted. "Ahmed. You're being rude to our guest."

He looked abashed. "Sorry, Emily."

"Food Storage?" I said.

"He didn't mean you, Clint! Don't worry!"

"Who are you, anyway? I was so busy trying not to die during the abduction that we never really got introduced. I mean, I know the human names you've chosen for yourselves—good job, by the way, choosing common names that won't attract attention—but am I allowed to know who you really are? What's your mission?"

"Sure, you're allowed," Emily said as Maria and Ahmed finished up with their work and stepped away to check readings on a bank of instruments.

"We need a baseline," Maria announced.

"I'm going to answer your question, Clint," Emily said, "but Antoine is going to ask you a bunch of boring stuff first before we get to the fun questions and answers, okay?"

"Okay." They did that sort of thing for polygraph tests. This seemed familiar, at least, if not normal. I was pretty sure I wasn't going to have a normal day again anytime soon, if ever.

They asked me where I was born, my favorite color, my mother's name, basic facts like that until Maria said she had what she needed.

"Excellent," Emily said. "So I'll answer your question now, Clint. We are from a star system about eight hundred light years from Earth, give or take, and in a few tens of thousands of years our sun will run out of hydrogen and begin to expand. Since our home world has an expiration date, we are actively looking for somewhere else to live and the clock is ticking. Our ship is one of many long-range scouting expeditions sent out to find an alternative, and happily, your planet began broadcasting on radio frequencies about a hundred years ago and we decided to investigate. We were already heading to a relatively nearby system that your astronomers have designated Trappist, but once we got your transmissions a course correction didn't take too long, and now we are well on our way to completing our mission: Earth is a habitable planet with an abundant food source and your sun won't expand for another five trillion years."

"Interesting results," Maria murmured, staring at her instruments. "That stimulated chemical production."

"So you're going to colonize us?" I asked.

"Yes!" Emily performed a fist pump then pointed at me victoriously. "That is why I put you on reserve, Clint! You're a smart one. Say, did I do that fist pump right? These human gestures are endlessly fascinating but performing them in proper context is key."

"Yeah," I muttered, not giving a damn about whether she timed her fist pumps correctly. My breathing quickened but I tried to keep calm by thinking about physics. "We're accelerating at one gee—or close to it—and you're going to maintain that until we get halfway and then decelerate at one gee?"

"Yes. We watched some of your science fiction and it's pretty great—though I guess we missed the shows featuring probes—but we don't have any fancy wormholes or gates between the stars. We just have the patience to think long term, and the rocketry and fuel problems your scientists think are insurmountable are in fact quite surmountable."

"I'd love to hear how you surmounted them. Still, even at constant acceleration, we're going to be traveling for centuries. That kind of distance will take eight hundred years or so."

"Not bad, Clint! But for us it will only be eight because of time dilation."

"Still, eight years of constant propulsion in a self-contained system? That would require enormous resources."

"Sure is lucky we have them, isn't it?"

I still had no idea how huge this ship was. I'd only seen the atmospheric craft that they used to get me off earth, and never got a look at the mother ship. While on board I'd only seen a small portion of it: my quarters and this lab room. But I might be able to get a sense of scale a different way. "Tell me about your food storage," I said.

Emily's eyebrows shot up in surprise, and then she glared at Ahmed. "See? He caught what you said and now he's obsessing over it."

"I'm very sorry," he apologized again. Emily grunted and her eyes slid back to me.

"You already saw what Janelle did to Derek. I think you're aware that we look at humans the way you look at chicken. You really want to see that?"

"Yes, I do."

She gave a tiny shrug and tapped at her tablet. "Okay. I'll just show you the holding areas. No need to see the onboard processing facility."

She stepped forward and swung the tablet around so I could see the screen. It showed a wide-angle shot of a large gray-walled room crammed full of naked people, all of them adults but still fairly young. That many people in close quarters immediately made me think of contagion—pandemic conditioning there— but I realized that a virus was not their immediate concern. Emily tapped the screen once every couple of seconds, a new image coming up each time, cycling through cell after cell, all full of people.

"My God," I breathed. "This is all on board? How many?"

"Fifty thousand healthy humans harvested from around the globe, a few decks below where we're standing right now."

I suppressed a shudder at the thought that we were being harvested. "You have eight years of food on board for fifty thousand humans and however many of you?"

"No, we have just a few weeks' worth of food for them. It's going to take us that long to get them butchered and frozen. And then they will be our food source for eight years."

"Oh God. You monsters."

"Now, now, Clint, let's be nice. Try to have some empathy here. I'm sure the animals of Earth think humans are monsters too. Don't hate us just because we're higher up the food chain." She turned to Ahmed. "I think he's ready."

"Right." Ahmed came forward with a metal clip attached to a wire and he reached toward my lap. Instinctively I tried to cover up with my hands, only to find that my arms wouldn't move off the armrest, and my legs were frozen too. There were no visible restraints, but I couldn't move.

"What is this? What are you doing? No!"

Ahmed attached the metal clip to some tender bits that definitely did not want an electrical shock.

"Aughh! Emily! You said you wouldn't violate me!"

The alien in a child's body threw her head back and laughed, and for the first time I saw all of her many teeth. There were three rows of them on both the top and bottom of her mouth.

I'm not going to relive what happened after that. Motherfuckers probed me.

—

I do, however, need to record what happened to Derek, because I think it will help me to write it down. I was interrupted before.

—

That unicorn girl—Janelle—obviously wasn't a girl at all. When she took off that hat and her wig, the noise that came out of her was not a scream so much as a high-pitched keening that was nearly ultrasonic. One of those alarm noises designed to annoy you, and simply not possible to make with human vocal cords.

And underneath that hat was not a nice bald scalp. The scalp wasn't even the same skin color as the rest of her: It was gray, and it was teeming with gray telescoping stingers, each about the thickness of a coaxial cable, and when she sprang forward those few steps and leapt into Derek's arms like he was her favorite uncle picking her up at the airport, those little bastards zipped forward and stung him multiple times in the face.

"Ah! Shit!" he said, and took two steps backward with the not-a-girl in his arms. Then his muscles all seized up because those stingers were full of paralytic toxin, and he fell over backward as wooden as a two-by-four as she rode him to the ground. He was alive and conscious and screaming as that mouth ratcheted open and tore into his chest.

"What the fuck! Get off him!" I swung my foot back to punt her, but Emily tackled me to the ground. She was a whole lot denser and stronger than she looked.

"Never interrupt a feed, silly," she said from atop my chest, and took off her hat and hair. I tried to punch her in the side of the head but she caught my fist in her hand and easily held it still. "We'll talk later." Those gray stingers whipped down at me and lit my nerves on fire as they lashed at my cheeks, and shortly thereafter I couldn't move. But I could see just fine, as Emily rolled off me and disappeared from my view, leaving me to stare up at the canopy of aspens softly whispering in the wind. I would have been able to appreciate their whispers more if I didn't have to listen to Janelle eating Derek right next to me, his screams thready and inchoate and eventually silent, though the chewing and gulping didn't stop.

I couldn't form words. I could only make despairing noises, so I made them. Derek and I had grown up together, gone to CU Boulder together. We had kids on the way, and our wives, Letitia and Candace, were hanging out together in Estes Park while we went hiking. Down on Main Street they had all these stores that made this ridiculous taffy, and I'd been looking forward to having some. We were going to eat a fancy dinner at the Stanley Hotel. But now Derek was lunch for some monster, and I was probably next.

That's when Emily's voice entered my ear on the right. I couldn't move my eyes to see her, but she was close.

"You know how this has to go, right?" she said. "You've seen too much. So there is no way you're headed home after this. There's no going back, only forward. But forward can mean all kinds of things. We can eat you too, for example, and shit you out later, and that will be the end of your story. Or you can join us and become one of the first humans to ever make an interstellar journey, see things you'd never see otherwise. Doesn't that sound better? And all you have to do is be patient and let the venom wear off, and then be cooperative when it's time to move. And by cooperative, I mean don't try to run or fight. We'll just take you down and paralyze you again, and then we'll drag you and you'll get gravel in your ass crack. Have you ever had gravel in your ass crack? It's the worst. You can't understand how bad it is until you've been there. It's something you have to experience, you know? Like listening to your friend get eaten right next to you. If I just said something was as bad as listening to your friend get eaten and it hadn't really happened to you, you'd shrug it off and say that sounded gross, and that would be it. But now you know how bad it is, so those words have true power now. Trust me when I say: You don't know the power of gravel in your ass crack. You don't *ever* want to know."

I didn't know how to respond. I moaned for Derek, for my lost future. Quantum physics suggested that there was a timeline where this hadn't happened to me, where we had taken a different trail and gone back to our hotels and our spouses and our blissful ignorant lives, but I was on the one where shit went bad, and I had no way of getting out of it.

"Are you full yet?" Emily asked Janelle.

The chewing and slurping sounds paused. "Not yet."

"Hurry up. We're going to have more hikers."

We would indeed. It was Labor Day Weekend and there were plenty of people visiting the park, the last great tourist weekend of the season, now that tourism was possible again. Four hikers did come along while Janelle was feasting on Derek, but Emily paralyzed them so they wouldn't be reporting the murder. I heard startled screams up the trail and then heavy crashes to the ground.

"We can't handle much more," Emily's voice called. "You need to be done whether you are or not."

"Fine. I'm done," Janelle said, half muffled because she was still chewing. "I *am* full, really. It's just that they're so tasty when they're fresh. I thought the frozen stuff was amazing, but oh! Mm. Gee whiz, as they used to say. Nothing beats this right here."

"That's why we brought you down. Everybody needs to try them fresh at least once. Now get rid of the carcass."

I was glad I couldn't see Janelle move Derek's remains, but I heard her drag him past me and then tumble him downhill. We were on a fairly steep portion of the trail, the hill dropping and ascending sharply from this bend.

Emily brought a five-gallon bucket out from behind a boulder that I spied peripherally before she dumped it over the spot where Derek had been killed. It was dirt and pine needles to absorb and cover up the blood, demonstrating that this ambush had all been planned in advance. The dust made me sneeze and cough, and the pinpricks of my motor control returning lit up my face. I was feeling the fire of the stings, too, which had faded shortly after they'd pierced me. I groaned in pain.

"Starting to feel it, mister? Good. The venom's breaking down and you'll be able to move soon. You can't form words or nod yet, so I'm going to ask you yes or no questions and you will answer eeeee for yes and ooooo for no. Vowels should be easy. Is that clear?"

"Eeeee."

"Great. First thing we need to establish is whether or not you want to live. We can do it either way, but it's up to you. Would you like to live, mister?"

"Eeeee."

"Yay! That makes me happy. So when you can get up and walk, I want you to get up and walk straight uphill. Don't run, mister. Don't shout. Just walk uphill. We are much faster and stronger than you and tend to get excited when prey flees, so running would be a very bad idea. If you just walk and cooperate like we discussed, I promise you'll be safe and eventually you might even be happy again. It'll be a different life than what you're used to, but it'll be a good one."

I had serious doubts about that. What kind of life did she mean? Life as a lab rat? A zoo animal? Whatever it was, I would certainly not be free.

"So I have two questions: Were my instructions clear?"

"Eeeee."

"Great. And will you cooperate?"

"Eeeee."

"I sure hope so. Because you humans are not only delicious, you're super funny and I like talking to you. Do you guys feel that way about cows? Nope—sorry, that was an insensitive question and I apologize. Okay. I'm going to step away to get these other hikers but we'll be watching. You'll be able to move very soon. Just walk uphill."

Once she left I had to decide whether I actually would cooperate. Because when you're paralyzed and a murderous alien asks you if you're going to cooperate, you say yes.

Running and fighting were options. I mean, watch out for the scalp-mounted stingers, right? Block with my backpack, kick the shit out of her, maybe. These creatures *did* move awfully fast and there was no denying she was strong. It's really easy to imagine kicking ass and you can believe it will happen the way you think it will right until the moment that your ass is kicked instead.

It sounded to me like these aliens had been doing this for a while. All summer, most likely. They knew almost exactly how long the venom would last— I could already wiggle my fingers and toes a few moments after Emily disappeared from view. They had been eating frozen humans on the mother ship—the existence of which I inferred by the fact that Emily had brought Janelle down for a taste of free-range human—so they'd been snacking on us for an extended period.

I could be next. I could get eaten alive and be tumbled downhill like Derek.

Or I could live and see what this life was that Emily was offering. Take this interstellar journey she was talking about. It might turn out to be wondrous. It might turn out to be worse than being eaten alive. I supposed there was only one way to find out.

If I did cooperate and just disappeared, someone would find Derek someday and they wouldn't find me. People would assume that I'd killed Derek and fled, because absolutely no one would leap to the conclusion that he'd been eaten by an alien and I'd been abducted.

Would they test for DNA in Derek's wounds? What would they find? Would some dude in glasses report to a detective like they do on TV and say in a nasal nerd voice, "The results are truly bizarre, sir. The genetic material...is not earthly"?

I bet they had a better plan that that. The bodies—because I assumed there were many of them, judging by how smooth Emily was—would never be found. They probably had a pit down there at the bottom of the hill and just poured acid on everything.

I realized Leticia and Candace would be devastated. They'd never forgive us for never coming back. For having to give birth alone. And I couldn't fix it. I hoped Letitia would find some other guy to be a good father for our kid. My tear ducts confirmed that they worked just fine. And then feeling flooded back into my muscles and I could move.

I stood and looked at the spot where Derek had been killed. I knew there was blood under that carpet of dirt and pine needles, but doubted anyone hiking along would realize. They'd be looking around at the trees and appreciating the fresh air. The pine scent was intense through here and they might not even smell the blood.

Turning my gaze downhill, I saw Janelle trudging toward me with her cap and hairpiece back on her head. There was no sign of Derek, except for the blood coating her chin.

Back on the trail, the way Derek and I had come, there was nothing to be seen. But a short distance up the hill from there, Emily was standing with two prone figures on either side of her. It was a pair of hikers she'd paralyzed and she was dragging them uphill by the straps of their backpacks. She was staring straight at me, waiting to see what I'd do.

I could try running down the trail and try to make it to the bus stop that shuttled people down the mountain to the parking area, but I was pretty sure I'd never even get close enough to shout for help. They wouldn't have left me so much room if they weren't confident that they could catch me. And they were watching. Expecting.

So I walked uphill. In the multiplicity of timelines threading and spooling throughout the universes, this was the Clint Beecham who chose to live a little while longer and see what happened next. Because, as Emily said, there was no going back.

"Goodbye, Letitia," I murmured as I walked. "Goodbye, kid. I wish I could be there for you." Letitia and I had not even picked out a name yet. Not knowing would be the absolute worst part of being this particular Clint Beecham. And it would be the worst part for Letitia and the kid, too.

I had other regrets. I had really been looking forward to a musical next week—theatre was a thing again and people were supporting it. And there was a good movie coming out the week after that, and I'd been planning to take Leticia to one of those theatres where you get a reserved seat and they bring you drinks. And I was pretty sure that whatever life the aliens had planned for me, it wouldn't include any craft beer. Certainly no Left Hand Milk Stout from Longmont. There would be no more simple pleasures.

"Goodbye, loaded nachos," I said.

I kept adding to the list as I hiked up, getting winded, because making the list kept me from panicking. Emily, I noted, kept pace off to my left, dragging two full-grown humans behind her as if they weighed no more than dry sticks of wood.

Janelle had picked up the other hikers somewhere and was trailing behind me and to my right.

I topped a rise in the hill where it leveled off before continuing to slope upward and beheld an alien atmospheric shuttle nestled snugly in the aspens.

From the trail it was utterly invisible; all one could and would see were ranks of marching tree trunks and leaves or needles. The chances of a hiker seeing it from below were absolutely zero. One would have to choose to trudge uphill for no good reason to see it.

It was not a pretty spacecraft, but it was silly to judge such things. It was abundantly clear that it was a functional spacecraft, far more advanced than anything humans made, and that was all that mattered.

The body had the shape, if not the color, of a warty pickle with stubby crescent-shaped wings. I imagined the warts were shielded sensor clusters. The color was the sort of drab off-white that a paint store might call *Raw Doughboy* or *Dyspeptic Eggshell*. There was some dome-shaped heat shielding on the front end and the engine housings bulged at the back end, giving the entire ship the unfortunate silhouette of a sad and lumpy cock and balls.

"They flew here in a dick ship?" I whispered.

At least there were no obvious weapons on it. But then again, the aliens themselves weren't into obvious weapons. They had already demonstrated that they liked to hide them. Looking up, I saw a net strung between tree trunks with aspen branches piled on top of it, a nice low-tech way to obscure the craft from satellite view.

A mechanical whirring noise drew my eyes back down. A door opened in the side of the craft and a ramp descended. Two aliens who looked like human adults descended, dressed in sporty outfits and baseball caps. They waved and beckoned to me. Emily came into view on my left and called out to them.

"That's the one on reserve! Don't eat him."

It was nice of her to make that clear.

We wound up meeting at the ramp. Emily had a paralyzed older man and woman in tow with sweatshirts that said NEW YORK on them. Tourists who'd come to see the Rocky Mountains and would never make it home.

"I have two for storage and Janelle is coming with two more," Emily said, dropping her burdens in front of the ramp. "So hey," she said to me. "What's your name, mister?"

"Clint."

"Hi, Clint. I'm Emily. Thanks for cooperating. You're smarter than most and that's what we need. Follow me inside and we'll get you situated and comfy, all right?"

She left the older couple lying there, paralyzed and grunting, and strode up the ramp. The two adult aliens bent to pick up the couple and drag them near the rear of the craft, and I watched until Emily prompted me to follow. I mounted the ramp and expected to see something like the interior of an airplane when I got to the top because I'd been conditioned for that all my life.

But I quickly remembered that human airplanes suck a lot—like, more than anything has ever sucked before—and there was no reason why aliens would choose to replicate that.

So there was a pleasant passenger lounge with ten plush oval couches built to withstand high-g acceleration. There was a human woman strapped into one already. She had dark brown skin like mine, natural hair, and wore a Buffaloes hoodie and black sweats with a gold stripe down the side, but she appeared to be napping and was buckled up. Emily gestured to the couch next to hers.

"That's Ayesha. She's a biologist from the university. You two can talk later, but sit here for now."

I noted that the other couches were empty. Were they planning on abducting a bunch of people with backgrounds in math and science and eating the rest of us? I talked as I moved.

"Emily, is there any chance of putting the hikers you paralyzed on reserve too, whatever that means? They're innocent."

"Innocent of what, exactly?"

"They don't deserve to be eaten."

"Neither did your friend, though, right? We're not here to judge you, Clint. We're here to eat you. When you go to a seafood restaurant and pick out a lobster to eat from the tank, do you weigh their sins and good deeds before you make a choice?"

"No, but—"

"No. Because you don't care about crustacean ethical systems. You don't care if they have ethics at all or whether one of them is a leading thinker of the lobster intelligentsia. You just want to dip them in melted butter. So you see what we have going on here."

"But you did judge me. You made a choice between me and Derek."

"True, but not based on ethics or whether you're innocent or anything like that. You know physics. At least you said you did. You weren't lying about that, were you?"

"No."

"Good. Sit."

I sat down and Emily asked me to get buckled up. The buckles themselves were a little strange, not steel and not plastic; they were some other kind of composite, but not all that different from restraints a human might have designed.

"We'll be leaving soon," Emily said, "so you won't have long to wait."

"Where are we going?"

"The far side of the moon. The Starscout—well, you would call it a mother ship—is hiding there."

"Why do you want a physicist and a biologist?"

"Let's circle back to that later. Time to sleep."

"What? I'm not sleepy."

Something punctured my left wrist. "Ow!" I raised it off the couch and saw a needle withdrawing into the fabric.

Emily leaned forward and said in a creepy, gravelly voice, "You will be. You *will* be." Then she drew back and smiled. "Ha! Did you see *The Empire Strikes Back?* That Yoda guy? He was great. I bet those movies really got on your nerves since they disregard physics. Aw, I can see you're getting drowsy now. Bye, Clint!"

I woke up in my quarters here, entirely missing my departure from earth, which was supremely disappointing. I mean, if I have to be abducted, at least let me find out if the lumpy dick ship provides a smooth ride.

My thoughts were slow and swimming in thick soup. I still didn't know why they chose to let me live. I didn't know if Ayesha was alive or what happened to those older hikers. Maybe they were among the fifty thousand waiting to be "processed."

I managed to sleep well last night because they drugged me, and I'm grateful for that small mercy, because if they hadn't I would have lain awake the whole time trying to figure out what benefit they got out of their fucking probe.

It's necessary for me to keep those journal entries, I think, especially to establish that I'm going to be cooperative without being suspiciously so. They have the benefit of being mostly true. It's true, for example, that I really would rather not be eaten and I will cooperate, since I have little choice. And it's therapeutic, getting those events out of my head and consigning them to paper. But Lord am I ready to take an opportunity to be uncooperative if it presents itself.

If it will take eight hundred years for us to get to the aliens' home world and report that there's a great new planet for them to colonize, that's a round trip of sixteen hundred years, give or take a few decades.

Humanity has that long to stay on top of the food chain, if it doesn't destroy itself by then.

I am sure there are all kinds of timelines in which humanity ruins the planet long before the aliens get back. Chances are good we are very likely on one of them, considering the accelerating rate of warming, the resultant extinctions, and the oligarchs and klepto-crats pushing us all off a cliff for their short-term profit.

But there might be some timelines where this scouting expedition never gets back to report, thereby allowing Earth to remain undiscovered a while longer. I want this timeline to be one of those very much, and I want to be the reason why.

If they haven't figured out faster-than-light travel there is no reason to suppose they discovered faster-than-light communication. They have to get much closer to home before sending any communication about Earth's location and superb qualifications for colonization. So all we have to do is figure out a way to defeat a species that has so far demonstrated hor-rific efficiency at hunting us, abducting us, and keeping their existence secret from the planet. Techni-cally we have eight years to figure it out, but functionally I'd say it's much less than that.

For one thing, I still don't know what they want from me and what they'll do with me once they get it. I'm not counting on them keeping me alive that whole time. Emily had lied about probing me, so I can assume she's lying about keeping me safe. I doubt very much that they have eight years of food for me and Ayesha and whoever else they've put on reserve.

For another, there are fifty thousand people in hold-ing cells who don't want to be food any more than I do.

They're probably being methodically butchered even now, and the longer I wait, the fewer allies I'll have.

They'd obviously been watching us and learning about us for quite some time—they spoke at least one language fluently, and I'm sure Emily's wasn't the only atmospheric craft that scooped up samples of snack food from the planet. The mothership had probably disgorged fleets of flying lumpy cocks. We had a lot of catching up to do. I don't even know what the aliens were called, much less the name of their language. Emily had neglected to tell me.

Not for the first time, I reflected that a nice convenient background in the martial arts would have served me well. Like, what if the aliens had tried to pull this shit on Donnie Yen? They'd be dead aliens. And in short order we'd be calling in an airstrike on their dick ships.

But lacking that—my hidden background was in long-distance cycling and collecting comic books, which gave me great legs and cardio health and the power to debate the merits of Stegron vs. the Lizard, and little else—my best bet was to find someone with combat training among the other humans on the ship. Emily had already demonstrated that she was more than capable of overpowering me.

Not that I was the proverbial ninety-eight-pound weakling. I carried a hundred eighty pounds on a six-foot frame and considered myself fit. I regularly went for fifty-mile rides on the roads of Colorado and flexed the calves of a god with every rotation of the pedals. I had stamina in spades. But I was not fit to go full John Wick on a mother ship full of aliens.

For a moment, I enjoyed a vignette in my head where I wore a skinny tie and stabbed Emily in the eye with a pencil. But then her stingers whipped down and stung my hand and I was paralyzed again and she began to eat me, so the moment of enjoyment was all too brief.

The room they had me in—a tiny gray cell—would yield me no weapons apart from the ill-suited pen resting next to my notebook. It would give me no armor, either, unless it was a pillow. That might shield me from stingers for a couple of seconds. In order to have a chance at defeating them, neutralizing the stingers would have to come first. A motorcycle helmet would be a good start. A cool mobile suit full of guns would be better. Or maybe something that sounded cyberpunk, like *armored plasgel*. But I didn't have any of that. Or did I?

Kneeling down next to the slab that served as my bed, I pressed my fingers into the smooshy gray foam on top, which was quite comfortable if unappealing to look at. Could this be removed, perhaps, and worn as a defense against their stingers?

Maybe. It might serve as makeshift body armor, but I couldn't breathe through it. I would still need something to protect my head.

Shifting my eyes to the edge where the mattress met the slab, examining the seam, a soft glow of actual color caught my attention. Something blue was shining from underneath the slab, so I peered underneath into shadow, and spied a blue square of light. What was that? A sensor? A power source? A self-destruct button?

Reaching into the shadow, I discovered that it was something much closer to me than the wall. There had been no way to judge depth. There was something under there that wasn't the wall. I felt for the edges, found them, and pulled. What emerged was a sort of footlocker with a glowing access panel.

There could be anything in there. Weapons. Shoes. Ice cream. An alien embryo waiting to attach itself to my spine and gestate inside my body. Mystery boxes in video games always hold loot, but in real life they can be terrifying.

Emily interrupted me before I could try to open it. The door to my room slid open and she said, "Clint, you silly! You're not supposed to open that yet. Come on, let's go meet the others. You can open it later."

"What's in there?"

"Stuff and things. You'll see later. We need you now."

"More probes?"

"Just light conversation. Come on. Ayesha's waiting." She waggled her eyebrows at me as if to suggest I was expecting an amorous liaison with a total stranger. Did she think that human males and females just automatically mated when conscious and placed in close proximity to one another?

Maybe she did. I supposed a lot of movies might give that impression. She probably thought people regularly met in high-stress situations and no matter what else happened to them that day, when night fell and it was time to sleep, there would be only one bed to share and heavy breathing would shortly ensue.

Whatever. I did want to meet Ayesha, but not for any reason that would involve a significant eyebrow waggle.

We turned right instead of left this time, though the corridor had nothing to distinguish itself that way from anything else, except that it was slightly longer. We turned left and then right and I noticed that we met no one else on our brief journey. But it was as good a time as any to get a question answered.

"You never told me who you are," I said. "What do you call yourselves?"

"Oh! I didn't realize. Saying it in our own language would be meaningless to you, but the closest approximation we can make using human vocal cords would be *mishawan*. We are mishawan, and we speak Mishawan when we're alone."

"But that requires a different set of vocal cords?"

"Yes. Your vocal cords aren't capable of replicating our language. But we can shift back and forth as needed while maintaining this bipedal form."

Her inclusion of *bipedal* suggested that she was accustomed to being something else, which I filed for later. I remembered that when Janelle attacked Derek she made some incredibly high-pitched noises that might have been their native tongue. "You physically transform your vocal cords on the fly?"

"That's right."

"What's your home world called?"

"It would roughly translate to Gray Garden."

"Gray Garden. And your Mishawan name wouldn't translate to Emily?"

She giggled. "No, silly. My full name would be something like She Who Hunts and Devours Her Prey With Precision and Gustatory Delight. We tend to favor nicknames as a result. I think Emily's a great name. It sounds friendly, and I like to think I'm a pretty friendly mishawan. But here we are." She gestured to a door that slid open for me and a much larger room than any I'd been in before waited. This one was painted an almost blinding white and was furnished with matching furniture that looked like it had been 3D-printed to human specifications. The cushions of the chairs contained the same gray foam gel that comprised my mattress. There were six of them, arranged in a circle, and five were already occupied by other humans, including Ayesha. All wore the same clothing as I did that bore the Mishawan admonition not to eat us. Standing behind each of the humans' chairs were more of the aliens—easily distinguished now by their ball caps, wigs, and too-large eyes.

"Have a seat, Clint," Emily said, standing behind me. "Welcome to the Reserves."

DAY 3, STILL, BUT LATER: NERVOUS DISTRIBUTION

Earlier, during what I'll call midmorning since it was a couple of hours after breakfast and also after I'd written my previous entry, Emily took me to a meeting of what she called the Reserves: Other humans, like me, who had been abducted but set aside from the fifty thousand others in food storage. There were six of us, all from scientific backgrounds.

Ayesha Powers was the biologist from CU Boulder who'd been brought up at the same time as me from Rocky Mountain National Park.

Hanh Vu was a marine biologist who'd been working near the dying Great Barrier Reef in Australia when she got scooped up.

Oscar Gastelo was a meteorologist from the Bay area, and Deepali Singh was a geologist from San Francisco who specialized in plate tectonics, so obviously there had been a dick ship near there, perhaps lurking in the Muir Woods.

Gregory Kincaid was a roboticist from some lab outside of Manchester, England, a pasty older fellow with a Vitamin D deficiency, and after we'd each had a turn at introducing ourselves to the group, he was the first to note one thing we all had in common: "It would appear we were all picked up in countries that use English as an official language."

"Yeah. Why is that, do you think?" Hanh asked. Her Australian accent was broad and welcoming, but she had her arms crossed defensively in front of her.

Emily stepped forward next to me and said, "I bet Clint can guess."

All eyes swung in my direction and I sighed. "They found us by picking up our earliest broadcasts in the twentieth century. A lot of that was in English."

"Correct!" Emily gushed. "Gosh, Clint, you're just super smart. Hi, everyone. For those of you who haven't met me yet, I'm Emily. I know I don't look like it to you, but as one of your actors might say, I'm kind of a big deal. Not an admiral so much as a captain, or its equivalent. The Reserves is my project."

If she was expecting applause at that point, we utterly failed to give it. We just stared at her in silence and waited. Captive audiences don't enthusiastically applaud until goaded and threatened.

She blinked her enormous orbs at us and looked around. "Don't you have any questions?"

Of course we did. We had all kinds of questions. But silence was a mood right then. And perhaps we all understood that the questions we asked would indicate what worried us the most. The act of asking would be giving them more information, and we didn't want to do that.

"Well. Then I'll explain a little, and if you have any questions, feel free to speak up." She moved to the center of the circle and spun around slowly as she talked. "Basically, we'd like each of you to share where you think the Earth will be in sixteen hundred years, as pertains to your area of expertise. So, Deepali—as an example—based on what you know of the planet's tectonic and volcanic activity, what might the Earth be dealing with in the next sixteen hundred years? More volcanoes? Anything falling into the sea, stuff like that?"

"Well, maybe," she replied. "You might have a new Galapagos Island by then. The west coast of Oregon and Washington may or may not still be there because of the Cascadian subduction zone. That could go tomorrow or it could remain there for thousands of years, but it's going to pop eventually."

"That's perfect! That's what I want to know. What might happen and the probabilities of it coming to pass."

Oscar squinted, a young man still in his mid-twenties who had probably landed a job at a local station right out of college due to his handsome face and expensive haircut. "Yo, I can't predict what the weather will be like sixteen hundred years from now. These days I have a hard time nailing down next week."

"Because the global temperature is rising fast and your baselines are almost meaningless?"

"That's right."

"Well, we want models of what the climate will be like more than local weather, so don't worry about that."

"I'm a meteorologist, not a climatologist."

"But you have some basic grasp of it, yes? You keep up with the science?"

"Yeah."

"That's all we need. The best work you can do."

Hanh spoke up. "What do you want from a marine biologist?" she asked.

Emily shrugged, a human gesture she must have picked up from watching television. "Will anything still be alive in the ocean, or will it be completely acidified and toxic?"

"Something will be there, sure. Depends on how badly we continue to pollute it and heat it up."

"Give us your best projections."

"Why sixteen hundred years?" Gregory asked, and Emily swung around and pointed at me with both hands.

"Clint! You're up!"

"Why you up again, Clint?" Ayesha asked. "How come you know everything already?"

"He figured it out," Emily answered. "He did the physics in his head! Did I mention he's super smart?"

"This is an out-and-back trip of sixteen hundred years," I explained. "But when they come back, they're bringing a whole lot of hungry friends. They're colonizers. They want to know what the world might look like when they get back."

"Sixteen hundred years from now?" Gregory spluttered. "Robotics will be so far advanced I wouldn't be able to dream of its capabilities."

"Not that this matters, but it won't be sixteen hundred years for us personally. For us it's eight years to get there, eight back."

"*If* we get back," Ayesha said, and I thought that was on point. I doubted any of us would get there to begin with.

"Yo, I'm not gonna model shit for you," Oscar said. "You want help colonizing us, count me out."

"Oh, hey, thanks, Oscar! I forgot to tell you all something," Emily said. "We left a couple of atmospheric craft behind. They're going to establish long-term bases for us underground. But they know where your families are on Earth and we're still in range to send them a message. So you can cooperate and your families will live out their natural lives, or you can be uncooperative and they will die now."

"Bullshit," Oscar said. "You don't know my family."

Emily consulted her datapad and tapped it a few times. She began reading names, some of them with Oscar's surname, some without. He paled, and Emily noticed.

"I guess we do know your family. So what's it going to be, Oscar? Do you want to help with some climate models and let them live?"

He didn't reply, biting his lip and eyes burning with hatred, but he nodded, once.

"Good. Does anyone else wish to opt their families out of living?" She looked around and we remained still, saying nothing. "Excellent. Then what do you need to prepare a report for us?"

"Paper, pens, and privacy," Ayesha said.

"Privacy?"

"Some time to talk amongst ourselves without you hovering behind us. You know we don't have weapons."

"We do. Because as you might imagine, you are under constant surveillance."

"So you should have no objections to my request."

Emily grinned, and I saw some of the others do the same. "You are correct. I do not."

"We'll also need a table. Circular, square, rectangular, whatever, just so long as we can sit around it."

"Done. We shall return with one shortly."

The aliens exited, leaving us alone, and Gregory spoke first. "Before you say anything, the surveillance is not a joke. They can hear everything you say and see everything you do." He waved his hand around at the walls and ceiling. "I can't tell you where the cameras and microphones are, but they are there. They conceal them like their stinger thingies on top of their heads. They're into concealment."

"What the hell are they, anyway?" Deepali asked.

"They call themselves mishawan," I said. "But that doesn't tell you *what* they are."

"They're cuttlefish," Ayesha said. "Space cuttlefish." She flicked her eyes over to Hanh. "Back me up here, marine biologist. They have all the essential properties, right?"

"I guess so?" Hanh said. "The paralytic toxin they inject before they eat you is certainly similar."

"But also the chromatophores in their skin, right?" Ayesha said.

Hanh's eyes widened in surprise. "Oh! Because they're mimicking us. They look like us."

"That's right." Ayesha gave her an approving smile but it faded when she looked around at the rest of us and saw blank expressions. "You saw the tops of their heads, right? Gray skin? That's what they look like normally. But the chromatophores let them change their skin color to whatever they want."

"But are they normally bipeds?" I asked. "Or are they something else? I got the idea that they might be something else."

"I won't know for sure until I cut one open," Ayesha said. "But I agree, I don't think they're normally bipeds. I think the only thing about them that's static are their eyes, teeth, and stingers. They can rearrange everything else."

"How?" I knew they could change physical structures internally because Emily confirmed that they did so with their vocal cords. But more than that was difficult to envision. "They just snap bones and regrow them?"

"No, I don't think they have an endoskeleton. They have a distributed nervous system and rely on cartilage. My best theory right now is that they're morphological mimics."

"Hold on, now," Oscar said. "A distributed nervous system?"

Hanh spoke up. "Cephalopods have a well-developed brain, but it doesn't handle everything. The arms of an octopus can act independently because they have a tremendous amount of nervous tissue in them. She's saying the aliens are like that."

"So if we shoot them in the head, they'll be fine?" Oscar asked.

"Well, not fine. But maybe not totally dead, either. And if they're able to move organs around, as Ayesha suggests, they might not be sheltering their primary brain in the head."

"Still, go for the head," Ayesha said. "You want them blind and unable to use their stingers on you.

Get those damn teeth out of action so they can't shuttle them elsewhere."

"What are you talking about?" Deepali asked.

"A lot of shit, but the short version is this: No bones means you can chop them up easily, so go for the neck."

"With what?" the geologist said. "I don't have a pocketknife, much less a battle ax at hand."

"Something for us to work on. Just thought you should know what you're dealing with if you have a chance to deal with it."

"Our chances are…not good," Gregory said. "The odds that we'll remain on reserve after we complete our projections are slim to none. There would be no reason for them to keep us alive once we've given them what they want."

"Agreed," I said. "Our window of opportunity is a small one."

"Guys? Maybe we shouldn't plan stuff where they can hear it," Deepali said.

"Where else is there?" Oscar asked.

The door to the room opened and Emily returned with two other adult-sized aliens who were carrying a round grey table. We made room as they placed it in the middle of our circle, and then Emily placed some notebooks and pens on top of it.

"There we go. And Oscar posited an excellent question. There is, in fact, nowhere you can go on this ship where we won't hear what you say. Plan whatever you want! We'll be ready. We've dealt with hostile prey before, you know. You're not the first and you won't be the last. You're undoubtedly the tastiest, though. Okay! Need anything else?"

Ayesha shook her head. "We'll call you if we do."

Emily giggled. "This part is super fun, you guys. You're going to try something stupid because you feel like you don't have a choice and you're right, you don't. But it's so amusing. And profitable! We have a pool going on which of you attacks first and whether or not you'll actually kill one of us. Good luck plotting your revolt! But don't forget to also do the work or your families die."

She and the other aliens exited, chuckling to themselves and smiling those toothy grins at us, and Oscar flipped his middle finger at their departing backs.

"Pinche culos," he groused.

"I'm starting to think we are merely shipboard entertainment," Gregory said. "Something to relieve the tedium of a long journey. They don't really require our predictions. Like I said, I cannot even conceive of where robotics and electronics will be in sixteen hundred years. I'd have difficulty imagining one hundred. And how can you even begin to predict physics, Clint?"

"Why bother picking up scientists, then?" Hanh wondered aloud. "If they wanted a military challenge instead of our predictions, why not pick up some veterans or active military?"

"They did," Ayesha said. "I'm ex-military."

"Me too," Oscar admitted.

"As am I," Gregory said. "Though obviously of a different generation and much further removed from my service."

"Shit," Deepali said. "So we *are* entertainment."

Hanh nodded. "Bastards are just playing with their food."

Ayesha raised a finger. "Speaking of which: Did y'all get probed? Because I got probed yesterday. They said they weren't planning on it but then they realized we had an expectation of it as a species and they just wanted to satisfy our cultural kink before they got to the important stuff. What the hell was that?"

"Yeah, they said that to me also," Deepali remarked, a haunted expression on her face. "Weird."

"I told them I did *not* expect that shit and even if I did they should defy my expectations and leave my sack alone," Oscar said.

"They did you too?" Ayesha asked.

"Yeah. Don't know who gave them that idea."

"Uh. That might have been me," I said. "Sorry."

Ayesha's eyes flared bright with anger. "You the one told them we expected to be probed, Clint? They put a metal clip on my hoohah and ran a hundred volts through it."

"Look, they got me too. I'm sorry."

I was immediately the least popular human on board and told my ass would never be forgiven for that shit.

Ayesha shook her head and distributed the notebooks and pens. "Let's get to work. We have two objectives: Save our families and kill these motherfuckers even though they know we gonna try."

We wrote out some predictions and wrote out some messages, too, shielded underneath our hands to thwart hidden cameras and also in code, to plan a course of action against the mishawan. I predicted we'd solve those insurmountable fuel problems and have our own long-range ships, plus energy weapons since I saw no reason not to lay down some wild speculation. There wasn't much else I could predict, and we all suspected the predictions were a pointless exercise. They really wanted us to rebel for their own sadistic entertainment.

This journal has been a good exercise for me. But I'm not writing down our planned course of action here. Because fuck you, Emily, that's why. You may know we're planning something, but you won't know what it is until it happens.

THE MYSTERY BOX

The mystery footlocker that I'd pulled out from my bunk was waiting for me when I returned from the meeting of the Reserves, and Emily told me I could open it now. I very purposely did not open it because she clearly wanted me to. Instead I wrote what I imagined would be my last entry in my journal, and only then did I kneel down to the box and examine it.

There did not appear to be an external latch or lock. I pressed my thumb experimentally to the blue light and was rewarded with an internal click as the lock disengaged and the top slid away. Was it biometric or heat-activated? I supposed it didn't matter. Inside were four items:

- A map of the ship (accuracy unknown)
- A key card
- A heavy straight-bladed dagger of the sort I believe would qualify as an Arkansas toothpick
- A note

I opened the note and found a handwritten missive:

Hi, Clint!

The key card will open any door on the ship, I promise. The other Reserves have the same information and materials.

You were ambushed before, but we don't want you all to die without being given a fair shot. We do want you to die, though. Just in a way that we'll find entertaining and be able to laugh about later.

The probes turned out to be super funny, so thanks for giving us that idea. We never would have thought of that on our own but the whole crew has been enjoying the videos we took. The rest of the fun begins whenever you wish. Open the door to a shipload of adventure! (Did I write that pun correctly? It was supposed to remind you of shitload. Your language is really amusing.)

Eat ya later,

Emily

I grunted in wry amusement. Ayesha had predicted we would be presented with something very similar to this—a weapon and an open door. What we would not be given was a chance to coordinate beyond that single meeting we had, or a chance to communicate with each other. The key to figuring that out had been Emily's slip in mentioning the pool regarding which one of us would attack first.

They want us to attack separately, impulsively, Ayesha had written in secret during our meeting. *So we will attack in concert according to plan.*

We had no reliable way to keep time except for meals, which arrived in our rooms via a slot in the wall at regular intervals. The cue to leave the room was dinnertime.

Hanh was pretty sure that she had passed a door leading to a stairwell on her way from her cell to our meeting room. We had all pooled our knowledge to create a rough map of the deck we were on. We were to meet at that theoretical stairwell when dinner arrived.

I left the note, card, and knife in the box and took the map back to my desk and spread it out.

The mishawan Starscout was miles long, and almost all of that was for fuel storage. We were in a relatively smaller portion up front. There were recycling plants for water, air, and waste. An entire deck of freezers for meat, since they were carnivores. And I had read all that before realizing that the entire thing was labeled in English.

They'd made this map especially for us.

Proof that they were being fair, perhaps? More likely it was an exercise in giving us hope so that they could enjoy taking it away from us later.

The bridge, I noticed, was up several decks and forward. The engine room was literally miles away. But how accurate was this map? Was it, for example, leaving out all the security measures? Or stairwells?

I searched for the stairwells and noted that there were several, as well as lifts, connecting the various decks. Which one were we on?

It took a while to find something recognizable, but eventually I located our meeting room, the space I had come to think of as the Probe Lab, and our respective cells, and their relationship to the stairwell Hanh had identified. So this ship map was accurate on our deck, at least. We were on Deck Four of ten; the bridge, comms, and landing berths for their atmospheric craft were on Deck One, Recreation was Deck Two—a vast open space as far as I could tell— and crew quarters were on Deck Three. Our deck was labeled as Medical and Science but that made me wonder about these cells and the meeting room. Were the decks as malleable as the bodies of the mishawan? Perhaps so. Deck Five was Material Synthesis and Life Support—lots of backups and auxiliaries there. Deck Six contained Water Recycling and Heating, and Deck Seven held Air Recyling and Food Processing.

Deck Eight was Live Food Storage, and Deck Nine was Frozen Food Storage, just a deck full of freezers where fifty thousand mechanically separated human parts would eventually be stored for later. These decks might have been devoted to hydroponic gardens and dry food storage on a human ship, but carnivores just needed the meat. Deck Nine included a kitchen and food service, which I took time to study as it appeared there was no mess hall. The mishawan preferred to have their meals delivered through lifts, and while the actual schematics were not included, I knew for a fact they delivered food up to Deck Four and doubtless to Deck Three, if not to Deck One itself. They had to do that through lifts somewhere, and those lifts—those shafts through the structure—would probably not be observed. Whether they were large enough to permit human travel was a question I'd dearly like to know. I didn't think I could fit through the food dispensing unit in my room and access whatever lay beyond, but maybe Deepali could. It would definitely be a tight fight.

Deck Ten was little more than a broad cargo hallway leading to multiple additional atmospheric craft of a different design than the dick ships and then some storage areas. It had egress to the massive fuel storage area, so I theorized that they brought up replacement fuel from planets or asteroids in those craft; they probably had mining capabilities.

There were, unfortunately, no helpful labels explaining what fuel they used, precisely, nor how their engines were built, because even with all that fuel, they'd still need tremendous efficiencies in the engines to make this doable.

One absence from the map that I noted in particular was anything marked Armory or remotely connected to weapons. Either they were purposely redacted or they didn't exist. I had not seen the mishawan use weapons up to this point, other than their stingers and teeth, but that did not mean they did not possess them.

A soft chime and a whooshing noise announced the arrival of my dinner, the contents of which I ignored. It was time.

I folded up the map and stuffed it into my back pocket. I retrieved the knife and key card from the footlocker and then used the knife to puncture my bed's upholstery and see what it was stuffed with. Turned out to be a dense, gelatinous foam—gray, of course. I sawed at the outer material to widen the gap and then plunged my hand in there to see if I could force my way into it and test its consistency. It was quite resistant, but it did compress well. I realized that I could compress it to the point where my arm could fit in there between the fabric of the mattress and its stuffing.

This was going to be my armored plasgel. I hastily cut out a square of the mattress to form a rudimentary shield and hoped it would stop the mishawan stingers. I very much doubted I'd be spending another night in that room.

TAKING NAMES

Derek used to have theories he would share with me over a beer. After we graduated from CU Boulder and got jobs—this was before the pandemic—we'd meet once a week at some craft brewpub, try something they had on tap, and he'd lay another theory down. Sometimes these theories were harrowing mashups of science and popular culture, like his idea that *The Princess Bride* was science fiction set in the distant future where we'd reverted to monarchies, and climate change migration would lead a startling number of people to be unemployed in Greenland. Or he would take something from literature and expand on it. He said one of the most provocative things that Shakespeare ever wrote was having Juliet ask, "What's in a name?" But the follow-up about roses and Montagues got all the attention.

"But a name is a necessary prelude to love," he said. "I don't mean love for all mankind. That's a nice phrase people throw around to mean they possess a sense of goodwill. Because how can you love all mankind? Some of them are dicks. Like Gary."

I chuckled and agreed.

"I'm talking real love here, platonic or otherwise," Derek said. "To get to a place of real love for someone, you have to learn their name. That's a crucial stepping stone. You can be attracted, you can be walking down that road, but at some point you have to say their name and it becomes real. More intense. Without a name, there's a distance, and you try to close that distance by learning their name. That's why Juliet asked the Nurse to find out Romeo's name. And I think it's why we can feel empathy for strangers in rough times, but we don't risk ourselves for them. Maybe we make a small donation to a relief charity when a hurricane hits, or maybe we try to reduce our carbon footprint to help out the vast sea of humanity. But we don't lay it on the line like we do for people that we actually know and love."

I was thinking of Derek's words because I loved him; he'd been a brother to me as much as a friend. And I was thinking of Letitia, the love of my life, and our unborn child who didn't have a name yet but whom I loved anyway. But I was also thinking of the fifty thousand strangers a few decks down, who all had names and dire circumstances but no relief charity to help them out. The only hope they had was the Reserves: Clint, Ayesha, Hanh, Deepali, Oscar, and

Gregory. I would fight with them and for them, kick ass or die trying, and when we got to Deck Eight, we would take some names. If we were all doomed, then no matter how corny it sounded, I wanted to call those people by their names and tell them they were loved.

DEREK'S COROLLARY

He took a swig of beer and waggled a finger at me. "The corollary—or whatever, I should know a better word, but this beer is 6.9% ABV—the corollary is that you don't need a name to hate someone. *Those people* or *that one guy with the beard* will work just fine. Or you can come up with a name for whoever you want to hate super fast, or use a handy racial slur, misogynistic term, or whatever. In fact, when haters are gonna hate, you'll see assigned names being used more often than their actual name, because that is a way to dehumanize them and imply that they don't deserve to be—urrrp, excuse me—loved."

That was true. We saw it in our politics on a daily basis and I was guilty of it myself. I didn't have a hater name for the mishawan yet but didn't think one was necessary. I was fully capable of hating them without coming up with some dissociative language that didn't already exist. They were aliens. Predators. They were going to eat us and they specifically wanted me and the other Reserves to die in an entertaining way. With my improvised mattress shield on my left arm—armored plasgel—I opened the door to my cell with my key card and drew my Arkansas toothpick. I peeked out into the hallway. Clear.

But I had no illusions that my movements were unobserved.

Moving quickly at a light jog, I took the turns required to get to that stairwell Hanh had seen and which had been marked on the map. That was our rendezvous point. Nothing leapt out at me on the way there. But when I turned the last corner and looked down the gray corridor, I saw bodies on the floor.

✳

There were two bodies, to be precise, but the rest of the Reserves were already there, spread out around them in a protective circle, except for Ayesha, who was kneeling down next to one of the prone forms. Hanh said, "There he is," when she spotted me.

One of the bodies was Oscar, and the other was mishawan, but unfortunately not any that I recognized.

"Is he…?"

"No, just paralyzed," Gregory said. "The alien jumped us and stung him and would have gotten Ayesha, too, except she had the same idea you had." He gestured at my makeshift shield. I saw something similar on the ground next to the mishawan body. Ayesha was using her knife to slash open the shirt it was wearing to expose the torso.

"Look at this shit," she said, pointing to a rather surprising anatomy. From underneath what would be the clavicle down to the belly button, the creature was little bigger than a mailing tube, a nearly literal stick figure in gray. "They have to stretch to make themselves look like adult humans. Conservation of mass means they can't change their weight much, so they give themselves shoulders and hips to fit human clothing but save where they can."

"So don't go for the chest. You'll probably miss," Gregory said.

"How'd you get this one?" I asked, though as soon as I did my eyes landed on the alien's head and the answer was obvious.

Ayesha said, "Just stabbed it in the face and twisted the blade around like a stir stick, scrambled everything. No bones, like I said. Heads are like grapefruits. Might even squirt you in the eye. You could probably squash them with an elbow."

"So that is why Emily chose to look like a juvenile. Smaller size meant she wouldn't have to stretch herself thin."

"Yeah."

"So where are the organs?"

Ayesha sliced open the alien from belly to groin—which was bare, the mishawan not bothering to reproduce human genitals—and peeled back the gray skin to reveal bruised purple flesh and indigo blood.

"Oh. Ulph. Ew." Deepali said, covering her mouth.

Ayesha flashed her a glare. "You better not spew on me, girl. If you're squeamish you need to get over that real quick. That goes for all of you."

"There's a reason I studied rocks," Deepali said, shutting her eyes. "No blood or juices or fluids."

"We don't have time for your hangups here. Ha, you see that?" She poked around at various bulging sacs in the cavity. "This one has its heart, lungs, and stomach crammed in the pelvic area. I bet a lot of other stuff is waiting in the legs, distributed among the muscle tissue. If you can't hit the head of an adult, the pelvic region is probably your best shot at hitting something vital."

"Why didn't it, uh…" Deepali trailed off.

"Why didn't it what?"

"Change back to its natural form when it died?" she finished in a tiny voice.

"Because that shit only happens in werewolf shows. When motherfuckers die their bodies don't keep chugging along doing acrobatic biology. They stay in whatever shape they had at the time of death."

"Sorry."

Ayesha softened, realizing she might have been a bit harsh. "Aw, don't worry. I know this ain't your wheelhouse. I sure don't know jack about rocks. Sorry for snapping at you."

"We should probably get moving," Gregory said. "Before reinforcements arrive."

"Right. I'll take point," Ayesha said, picking up her mattress shield and shoving her arm inside.

"What about Oscar?" Hanh asked.

It was clear to me that as the largest individual remaining I'd have to carry him, so I volunteered for the duty, handed my knife to Deepali, and gave my shield to Gregory so he could act as rear guard.

"Come on, buddy," I said, hefting him up and tossing him over my shoulder in a fireman's carry. "Can't guarantee the ride will be pain-free and it certainly won't be smooth, but we'll get you downstairs and hopefully that venom will wear off soon."

"I have his knife," Hanh said, so we were set. The stairwell doors were unsecured, which is why we had decided to use them before we even knew that we'd be getting key cards. Ayesha opened it to take a quick look up and down.

"Clear," she announced. "Let's go."

Hanh followed after her with two knives, I carried Oscar next, and Deepali and Gregory brought up the rear.

As we descended and I saw the alien script on the back of Hanh's shirt, it occurred to me that it might not say DO NOT EAT as Emily had told us. In all likelihood that had been another one of her lies. It probably said A SNACK FOR LATER or HOT AND FRESH or even OKAY TO EAT IF UNACCOMPANIED BY MISHAWAN.

"Deck Five," Ayesha said as we passed a sign above a door on the next landing. The sign wasn't in English, but we could make a fine guess at what it said based on context.

When we got to Deck Six we heard a door open somewhere above us and the high-pitched whistling sounds of the mishawan.

By Deck Seven Gregory had spotted them. "Two coming behind us," he called.

Ayesha hurried down to Deck Eight, feet thudding on the metal stairs, and Hanh kept pace. I could not hurry because Oscar weighed almost as much as me and my knees were complaining that they had to carry twice the load. Deepali did not appreciate this.

"Come on, Clint, they're moving fast!" she cried, terror scratching her voice ragged. "Can't you hear them?"

"This is my top speed right here," I said. "You'll have to fight them off."

"I'm not a fighter and I'm definitely not a killer. I'm vegan."

"The mishawan are *not* vegan, though, and they will eat you," I said over my shoulder. "So your choices are to kill them and get some therapy later or to be paralyzed and eaten alive. I wish it wasn't true, but that's the reality."

"Good talk, Clint," she said, her voice suddenly hard. "But also fuck you."

"Face them with me on this landing," Gregory said, the noise of the alien steps pounding the air above us and their high-pitched hoots grinding in our ears. I was heading down the last flight to Deck Eight when the door ahead burst open just as Ayesha was reaching for the handle. Two mishawan in childlike bodies leapt at her, and she held up her shield in front of her face and stabbed underneath it with quick thrusts. I kept moving, since I couldn't get in the fight until I got Oscar off my back. But then I heard more alien cries and Deepali's scream behind me and I turned to see what happened, dread robbing me of breath.

The geologist was already collapsing backwards with a mishawan on top of her, stingers having pierced her face and the toxins beginning to lock up her muscles. Despite her reluctance to harm any creature, she had plunged one of her knives into its throat, and that kept it from finishing her off as it dealt with that.

Gregory was fighting a new horror that I could only assume was a mishawan in their natural state. It was a quadruped, entirely gray-skinned and unclothed, its body built like an overmuscled bulldog with talons instead of claws, the eyes, teeth, and stingers instantly recognizable on the square-jawed head. The teeth weren't hidden by human lips anymore and were much more prominent; the nose was not on a snout or any fleshy appendage but rather three teardrop orifices centered below the eyes. Ears were pointed and swept back on the sides, but looked like they could rotate and billow out as needed.

Gregory effectively blocked its stingers with the mattress shield I'd given him and stabbed repeatedly, which tore some shrieks from the mishawan.

That let the other one in human form know that there was trouble and it decided to help out even though it had a knife in its neck.

I needed to help out as well. I heaved myself and Oscar up a few steps as the human-shaped alien turned to Gregory and lashed those stingers at his leg, lancing through his pants and delivering venom into his thigh.

"Ow! You bastard!" Gregory cried out, and flipped his grip on his knife so that he could stab down at the mishawan's face. But it blocked the strike with a hand, simply waiting for the venom to bring the man down. The doglike one was expiring, still alive but just barely, breathing indigo blood bubbles and taking the opportunity to retreat back up the stairs. Gregory crumpled, totally vulnerable as Deepali was, and I had no weapons to help them out.

Nothing except the hundred and sixty pounds of Oscar.

"Sorry about this, buddy," I muttered, and threw him with a grunt at the mishawan. He landed with a thud on top of the creature, flattening him so that he was the meat in a human sandwich, Deepali and Gregory on the bottom and Oscar on top. There was some thrashing and Oscar wouldn't remain there for long, but it gave me the chance to grab Deepali's other knife—which was actually mine—and shove it into the base of the alien's head.

It really did feel like slicing into a cantaloupe or grapefruit, just a tiny bit of resistance and no bones. I twisted the knife around to make sure it died, and then climbed over everyone to finish off the doglike one halfway up the next flight.

An alarm abruptly blared and the lights in the stairwell turned red. Our small victory had apparently been observed. A mishawan voice keened a garbled bunch of high-pitched syllables, and we would no doubt be facing a concentration of security in short order. And we were down to three mobile fighters now.

"Help me get them downstairs!" I called to Ayesha and Hanh.

"You go," Ayesha said to Hanh. "I'm securing the door."

That was a good call. Wouldn't do to be ambushed from behind.

"Again, my dude, I'm sorry I had to toss you like that," I said to Oscar as I hauled him up off the dead alien. I knew he could hear me. "I hope I didn't hurt anything. That venom will wear off soon and you can cuss me out if you want."

I hauled him down and Hanh squeezed past us to get Deepali. There was little room at the base of the stairs, so I had to prop Oscar up in the corner as best as I could. Hanh struggled to bring down Deepali but made it all right by hooking her arms underneath Deepali's and slowly backing down, letting the geologist's feet drag behind her.

I retrieved all three of the knives up there and slipped them inside the slit of the shield, then grunted as I lifted Gregory onto my shoulder. He was heavier than Oscar. I almost dropped him when something slammed into the door below and surprised the hell out of Ayesha and Hanh, followed closely by an earsplitting shriek.

"Hanh! Help me!" Ayesha braced herself even harder against the door and Hanh sort of dumped Deepali unceremoniously next to Oscar. As I tried to hurry down with Gregory, I realized that Deepali had no way to balance herself and Hanh hadn't taken enough care; the geologist slowly fell over sideways headfirst into Oscar's lap.

The pounding resumed and the door shuddered and the alien shrieks behind it were even louder. The door handles were lower and different than ones on earth, being a horizontal bar in a hollowed-out half sphere that could be rotated ninety degrees; if the bar was vertical, the lock was disengaged. The bar was vertical and it was all Ayesha and Hanh could do to keep it closed. They were stronger than us.

"Hurry up, Clint!" Ayesha said.

"I am!" Gregory's landing might have been a little less careful than I would have wished but I made sure he didn't crack his head on the wall and propped him up steadily. Then I grabbed a handful of Deepali's shirt at the shoulder and hauled her upright.

"What are you doing? Get over here!" Between the stress and the necessity to be heard over the alien shrieks and the ship alarm, Ayesha was shouting.

"I can't leave her like that!" Deepali might not have liked me for suggesting she murder sentient creatures and follow up with a therapy chaser, but no one deserved to be paralyzed face down in someone else's crotch. I could only imagine how embarrassed both she and Oscar must be feeling right now.

"Motherfucker we gonna die!"

"Well, if we do, we gonna die with dignity!"

With our three paralyzed friends situated, I pulled the knives out of my shield and left two of them for Deepali and Gregory.

"Okay, what do you want?" I asked.

"You go high, I go low, Hanh tries to keep the door mostly closed."

"What?"

"Just stand here where the door will open with your shield up, and when it opens, you stab that screaming bastard."

"Okay."

I put myself in position, shield up, and when Ayesha was satisfied, she turned and said something to Hanh I didn't catch. The pounding and shrieking continued. I glanced behind me at the stairwell to make sure no more aliens were coming down. Clear for the moment.

When I turned back, Ayesha spun away from the door and crouched down in front of my shins, facing the door, her shield up and her knife ready. She nodded at Hanh and the marine biologist spun as well, grabbing the door bar and yanking it open a couple of feet. It caught the alien on the other side off balance and it practically stumbled face first into my shield.

That was my moment, in the legendary cinematic parlance of Marsellus Wallace, to pop a cap in its ass.

Normally I don't even like to dress a whole chicken. Give me nuggets that don't look like anything, you know? Shapeless blobs are easy to eat and don't trouble me because they look nothing like a former animal that may or may not have enjoyed its life. But confronted with a mishawan, I found I had no hesitation taking a knife to it.

Maybe it was adrenaline. Maybe it was the fact that I'd had to listen to Janelle, the unicorn girl, eat my best friend. Maybe it was just ancient hunters' instinct asserting itself, the thin veneer of modern civilization dissolved by the acid of combat. Whatever it was, I felt like one of those cocaine hippos living in Colombia, ripped from my natural habitat but determined to survive and even flourish in my new surroundings, ready to murder anything in my way.

I thrust my knife underneath the shield, up through the bottom of the alien's jaw and into the brain. Ayesha didn't have a target since its body was lagging behind, but once I'd essentially killed it, she rose and pushed it back. Another alien that had been out of sight of the doorway screeched and leapt into its place, attacking right away by lowering its head and thrusting those paralytic stingers at us. It met the combined wall of our mattress shields, the gel foam inside compressing and halting the stingers, but one slipped through the gap and managed to tag Ayesha on her upper left arm. She cursed and let me know she might freeze up.

But the mishawan was vulnerable after that, and I took the opportunity to shove my knife through its brain. Its screeching ceased and I knocked it backward away from the door, peeking out to see if any more were incoming. There was a wide gray hallway lit by red lights but no more living aliens visible.

"Clear for the moment," I said. "Ayesha, you okay?"

"Arm's numb, but that's it. Not enough juice in one stinger to take me down. Let's go. We gotta get across that hallway. Hauling three bodies is more than I thought we'd have to deal with."

The hauling of bodies was something we'd agreed upon first thing: We knew that they'd paralyze at least one of us, at minimum, and we had all pledged to protect one another while in that state as we followed the plan. In this scenario, I'd be doing all the actual hauling. Hanh remained on guard in the stairwell with my shield to fight anything coming down the stairs; Ayesha went with me and my first cargo, Gregory, diagonally across the hall to a corridor we believed was full of detention cells.

When we'd been in the meeting room, the plan we'd worked out via the painstaking passing of notes was to go down, not up, once we had the chance, since we knew from my probe session that the prisoners were housed somewhere below. The mishawan would expect us to rush the bridge with six knives between us, and everyone agreed that would be strategically unwise. Rushing the bridge was ultimately necessary, of course, but we figured we needed to complete a whole raft of side quests first. Like getting some help, and hopefully some better weapons. Taking as many of the aliens with us as possible was also high on our list. So the plan was: Get to the unsecured stairwell at the dinner bell, go down to free as many prisoners as possible, and then improvise from there.

The fact that the mishawan had given us weapons, key cards, and a map of the ship was far more fair play than we'd expected. I wondered idly if Emily was entertained yet by the deaths we'd tallied so far. And I wondered what triggered the alarm, because it wasn't the first mishawan death. My private theory was that they hit the alarm when they realized we were not only acting in concert but had a goal that didn't involve the bridge. They hadn't concentrated their defenses down here.

I dropped Gregory out of sight from the wide hall-way in a door niche that led to a detention block—or rather the area marked Live Food Storage. Ayesha remained with him and examined the door, which was a secured one that would require a key card. It had a window in it and she peered through, but I didn't stick around to hear what she saw. I had two more people to drag across an exposed area before alien reinforcements arrived, and I felt sure they had to be arriving soon.

When I opened the stairwell door, I heard them coming from above, and Oscar was struggling to his feet, the venom wearing off. That meant we only had to drag Deepali away.

"Okay, good. Hanh, you take Deepali and get across to Ayesha. Give me the shield. Yeah. I've got your back."

There were more than two mishawan coming down the stairs now, judging by the sound of it. I held the door open and Oscar staggered across the hall to Ayesha and Gregory. Hanh followed, holding Deepali under her arms and dragging her feet behind. And I realized that even with a shield, I wouldn't last long against multiple aliens with no backup, especially when they could attack from high ground. There were three of the chirping dog-like ones rounding the corner of the landing, and that is when I figured that the bottom of a stairwell is a senseless hill to die on, especially since there was no hill.

I scooted out into the hall and shut the door in the leader's face, turning the handle horizontal and leaning all my weight on it, hoping they wouldn't be able to wrest it open.

Whether they pressed through or some others came and found me there in the hall, struggling with the door—a distinct possibility, as I heard some of their vocalizations coming from around a corner—I was alone and exposed.

EMILY TV

The hidden cameras that Gregory had posited were everywhere also extended to hidden monitors. As the mishawan alternately pounded at the door and tried to turn the handle open, a square portion of the surface rippled and smoothed out and then flickered to life.

"Hi, Clint!" Emily said. She was beaming radiantly at me as if we were close friends instead of a predator who'd promised to eat me later. She had no right to smile at me like that.

"Hey, fuck you, kid," I said, and grunted as the door handle nearly slipped out of my grasp and unlocked. I dropped my shield and placed both hands on it, white-knuckled, the left pressing down and the right pushing up to keep it horizontal.

"Just wanted to thank you for surprising us and keeping this interesting. Humans can be clever when they're not being ambushed, and we needed to know that. Couldn't really do something like this on your planet and guarantee operational security. Too many variables and unpredictable results, as you've aptly demonstrated. Well done."

"I thought you watched a bunch of our movies and stuff. Studied our history. You should have figured it out from that."

"Yes, well, the movies are fiction, aren't they? Stories you like to tell each other involving stuntmen and a script, and most of the stunts are digitally manipulated fantasies. Doesn't mean you can do anything real."

"We're really pretty good at war."

"Ehhh, not so much, lately. Last time you really got into it was generations ago—you called them the Greatest Generation, isn't that right?"

"I'm a millennial and we destroy all kinds of shit. Just ask the boomers."

"I saw some of that discourse and didn't really understand that. Seemed like a lot of shouting about avocado toast. But kudos for improvising that shield, Clint, and again, I wanted to deliver a sincere thank-you before we eat you. This is fantastic intel. All this stuff you're doing is going to help us develop security protocols for colonization later."

"What I'm doing is kicking your ass."

"Are you, though? You've managed to kill five unarmed mishawan when you outnumbered them and have yet to face a serious assault."

"You telling me the mishawan trying to get through this door aren't serious?"

"They're seriously hungry," Emily said, and then giggled and said something I missed because distractions abounded.

"What was that?"

"Oh, you're having trouble hearing. Hold on a second." She turned her head to the side and spoke to someone off camera. "Kill the alarm." Behind her I saw some monitors and panels with buttons and lights on them. She might be on the bridge. The alarm ceased and the red lights returned to their normal white. I could hear the shrieks of the mishawan behind the door much better now, as well as those who were converging from elsewhere on the deck. Four figures appeared down the hall on my left, human shapes with ballcaps on their heads, and one of them pointed me out. To my right, five mishawan dogs rounded the corner and ululated. Emily hummed with pleasure. "I said we have you outnumbered this time, don't we? You shouldn't worry about them too much, though. They're just going to paralyze you. They're allowed to eat the others, and they're supposed to eat them where you can hear if possible, but I'll be the one to eat you, Clint. You're on reserve, after all. Bet you're tasty as all fuck."

I have never wanted to obliterate a sentient being so much as at that moment. I prayed a most urgent and holy prayer for a death ray or a nuclear warhead or a nice barrel of napalm and the chance to use it on Emily.

"How do I change the channel?" I said, and Emily laughed as the door bucked and twisted in my grip and the mishawan down the hall whooped in their glee.

MOB MENTALITY

Some high-pitched words offscreen caused Emily's smile to disappear. "What? Show me," she said, and the screen blessedly went dark. Whatever displeased her was just peachy in my book, and in the next moment I figured out what it was.

Ayesha had made it into the cell block and set some people free. A horde of wild-eyed naked people came streaming out of the detention area and filled the hallway, immediately blocking me off from the approaching mishawan on either side. A very large yet nimble young man, a nose tackle if I ever saw one, called to me to let the door go and get out of the way.

"Move, bro, we got this!" he said, and he was charging the door, so I trusted him. I let go of the handle and spun to the left, squatting down to pick up my shield and knife where I'd dropped them. The door flew open, a mishawan stepped out, and immediately got flattened by the nose tackle. More humans followed up and disappeared into the stairwell.

What we had was a murderous mob. Hundreds here, but thousands more coming. A bunch of people who'd been ambushed and kidnapped and forced into holding areas with no visible facilities to relieve themselves. They were filthy and pissed and hyperaware of the stakes: fight and maybe live, or don't fight and definitely die.

Time to improvise. My best move was to inform them.

"You're on Deck Eight!" I shouted. "The bridge is upstairs on Deck One! Secure all decks and move up!" I kept repeating that and heard others passing it on. Recalling that food processing was one deck above, I inserted a mention of that.

"Food Processing on Deck Seven! There may be knives or other tools there that can be used as weapons! Get the weapons! Kill them all! Fuck yeah!"

That, I surmised, would go down as one of the top things I never thought I'd say as a physicist. But all of my old ideas about what my life would be like had to be burned now. This was a different timeline from the one where Clint Beecham never got abducted, and here, "Kill them all" was exactly the sort of thing I would and should say.

I kept yelling as people streamed out of the detention hall and up the stairs or to either side. I searched for anyone with clothes on, because that would mean they were part of the Reserves.

"They're strong but they have no bones! You can crush their heads! Secure the doors of every floor so they can't lock us off from any deck! The bridge is on Deck One! You're on Deck Eight!" And so on, until a man paused in front of me. He was of South Asian descent and solidly built like me and every inch as tall, but he spoke with a British accent.

"Are you Clint?" he asked.

"Yes."

"Ayesha says to wait here. She's coming with Gregory. The others are going to keep setting people free and then they're going to—wait." He peered at the walls. "They can hear us, can't they?"

"Yes."

"Maybe not in the mob though. Come away from the wall."

We waded into the stream of the mob in the middle of the hallway and he spoke in my ear in low tones in hopes that they wouldn't be able to pick out his words from the rest of the noise.

"Oscar, Hanh, and Deepali are going to take a group and head for the engines."

"The engines? Why?"

"To either scuttle the ship or, if we succeed up here, to keep them from scuttling it."

I blinked. "I never would have thought of that until it was too late. I'm glad we have some military minds on this. You have experience?"

"Yes, I served in the Royal Air Force. Lieutenant Teddy Gopal."

"Teddy. It is awesome to meet you and I want you to know that I love you. I just wanted you to hear that from somebody today in case, you know?"

His eyes widened for a moment, then softened and he clapped me on the shoulder a couple of times. "I understand. I love you too."

"Thanks. So what next, Lieutenant?"

"Secure the stairwells. Cause chaos. Get you with your key cards up there because I'm sure they're locking themselves off. Wouldn't be surprised if they take that functionality away soon, so we need weapons or tools that can manually open the doors."

That was a good point. I doubted that Emily would continue to play by the rules once it looked like the mishawan might actually lose more than a few of their crew. She was probably reevaluating even now with the directive to future colonizers that humans should never be given a chance to fight back.

"But we're still gonna kick their asses, right?"

"Yes, of course. I think we must already outnumber their crew, even though not everyone's free yet."

"The alien who set this up wants to personally snack on my pancreas, so she'll be watching me at all times on whatever surveillance they have. If you want to do anything sneaky, don't do it around me."

"Oh, that's good to know. You're our distraction."

Ayesha and Gregory appeared by our side in the midst of the streaming mob.

"Good, you found him," she said to Teddy, then caught my eye. "Let's go, Clint."

"Where we going?"

"Upstairs."

PROCESS MATTERS

There were, of course, additional stairwells in the ship, and people found them, because Ayesha spread three basic directives as she released people from detention:
- Kill them all or we will all be killed.
- Use and secure the stairs; move up.
- Secure but do not use the lifts.

The last point was almost unnecessary because key cards were required to open them, but we didn't want someone finding an open one and trying to use it; once inside, the mishawan could easily override them from the bridge and usher them to an ambush. But we guarded them so that any forces they sent to outflank us would be trapped in a kill box.

Ayesha didn't take us to the stairwell that we'd used to come down; it was crowded enough as is and anyway we had a different goal in mind. She led us in the direction that the doglike mishawan had been approaching from, because there was a stairwell in that direction that led to the spot on the map marked Food Processing.

I nearly slipped on a slick patch of floor smeared with indigo blood and had to dance over the carcass of one of the mishawan. The mob had torn them apart, and there were some humans as well that were paralyzed and people couldn't really move them out of the way in such a mob, so we had to step around them instead.

It was disorienting to think of what all these people would be doing right now in another timeline where they hadn't been kidnapped. Maybe grabbing some coffee and donuts in a drive-thru on their way into work, battling traffic and wishing their mundane lives were different. Or maybe continuing their interrupted vacation, since I felt pretty sure the mishawan had chosen their targets outside of cities where they could simply disappear. They could be enjoying ice cream in a small mountain hamlet or listening to some of the last remaining birds on the planet. Instead they were mobbing aliens on an interstellar spacecraft.

Well, it was a more interesting day than anything they'd do at their jobs, to be sure. Certainly more likely to give their adrenal glands a workout. There was that.

We weaved past several knots of people that had formed around fallen mishawan and eventually made the required turn to get to the stairwell we needed. Once through the door, Ayesha told the people ahead and behind us that we were heading into the Processing plant to get weapons.

"It's gonna be some nasty shit in there," she said, "but that's where we'll find knives and saws and things."

We had no shortage of volunteers to accompany us. The door to the processing center looked no different than the others we'd seen; it was a sliding door secured with key card terminal on the right side.

"I don't know what's on the other side of this," Ayesha said, "so be ready for anything. Just take them out."

Gregory's card opened the door and several naked folks, Teddy among them, preceded us through the door.

Horrors awaited inside.

It was a large space, an industrial sort of operation similar to abattoirs on Earth. Humans were hung upside down on a line, ankles bound and a hook holding them up, their throats slit so that the blood would drain into waiting vessels that preserved it for soups or some other mishawan recipe. Organs were removed from the abdomen further down the line, sorted and packaged. Then meat saws shrieked as they sheared through bone, heads were removed and brains extracted, eyeballs preserved, cheek cutlets harvested, and ears sent to be dried for snacks.

We heard human screams in the back, people shouting "No!" and "Don't!" and so on. It was the beginning of the line, where they entered the slaughterhouse and were strung up, paralyzed before having their throats cut.

"Everyone to the back! Save those people!" Ayesha shouted, and we steamrolled along, tackling any alien that got in our way—my wild guess was that there were two to four dozen in the space. I fought one off with my shield and knifed it, and then turned a corner to where the screaming was.

A mishawan shaped as an adult human held a pronged instrument like a cattle prod, fitted with cylinders of venom on the side. He was using it to paralyze humans as they came out of a chute, pushed forward mechanically by a metal plate. That told me that the venom supply in their stingers was not infinite. A dog-shaped mishawan then took them as they fell, bound their ankles, and mounted them on hooks to be pushed down the line and slaughtered. That was taken care of by a couple more mishawan who wore blood-splattered aprons and wielded knives.

Taking that in took a fraction of a second, and it took another fraction for us to just lose our shit. Ayesha and Teddy and a good chunk of the others charged the guy with the venom prod; Gregory and I and some other newfound friends went after the guys with knives. They had morphed their legs to human ones for the work, but had kept their natural doglike torsos and toothy faces.

I had a knife too. And I knew from experience that knives would penetrate the mattress material, but it would certainly slow them down and perhaps prevent a fatal blow, so I led with it and felt the sting of the blade in my forearm as the slaughterer plunged his weapon into it.

My flesh wrenched the blade free of his hand, though, and he had no shield against my blade. My first thrust didn't hit home—he dodged and escaped with a scratch—and my second missed completely. His stingers were rearing back to strike me, but another human tackled him and took those stingers to the face, and I was able to finish him off at that point, as he couldn't dodge me when pressed underneath the weight of another.

"Thanks, brother," I said to the man who was freezing up, pulling him off the mishawan and sitting him upright against a rank of stacked blood buckets. He was a man about my size with warm brown skin, fit and cut and in his early twenties. "We saved some people there and you saved me too." I pulled the knife out of my forearm with a wince and grunt and laid it on the floor next to his right hand. "You earned this. My name's Clint. When the venom wears off you can tell me your name."

With the other slaughterer taken down by Gregory and a couple others, and Ayesha and Teddy's group having successfully slain the paralyzing duo, we were able to pull down five paralyzed but living humans from the hooks and set them down next to the man who'd come to my aid. More humans were being pushed through the chute, one at a time, and Ayesha recruited them instantly to "go forth and kill some motherfuckers."

We surged through the slaughterhouse floor, taking some casualties at first, sadly losing people whose names I would never learn, but we lost fewer as we went, picking up weapons as we progressed, and also some numbers as another fifty or so people got pushed through to be processed, only to discover we'd already saved them.

The meat hooks were perfect, piercing the mishawan flesh easily and tearing through their boneless tissue, doing maximum damage. The blood buckets, we found, made effective shields against stingers as well as a nice blunt force weapon. Gregory roamed the floor, examining the machines at various stations with a professional eye.

Once the facility was secure, I'd found some packing tape to plaster on my arm, and some of the paralyzed began to stir, I asked Ayesha what we should do next.

"Upstairs again," she said. "But this time we go to the top."

Fifty-plus armed and partially shielded humans had much better odds at surviving than six. And there were plenty more out there, swarming the stairs and making life hell for the aliens. Heading upstairs sounded like a great idea until we tried to exit the room. Both of our key cards failed to work.

"Shit, they've been deactivated," she said. "Guess we were getting too real for Emily. She's trapped us in here."

Emily must have been listening, for she appeared after that on a newly materialized monitor in the door. "Hi, Clint and Ayesha! I have good news and bad news! The good news is that we are really impressed with you humans now! You were so easy to ambush one or two at a time and your science was so far behind ours that we thought this would be easy, and some of us didn't even think the Knife Test was necessary. That's what we call this, by the way: The Knife Test. We do this whenever we're going to colonize. Some species just take that knife and kill themselves with it. Some go hunting for us all alone and kill as many of us as they can. But not humans! Wow, get you guys together and you're something else! You take that dial pointing to fear and obedience and turn it all the way up to murder spree. So that brings me to the bad news. We've learned what we needed to learn, which is that we really need to stick to ambushing you because your insurrection index is off the charts. That means the game is over. Your key cards won't work now, as you've noticed, so just stay there—like you have a choice, ha ha!—and we'll be by to exterminate you soon enough. You're off the Reserves and nobody's going to save you for later. But hey—good job, Clint! You're super smart, like I said, smarter than any food I've ever met, a real credit to your succulent species."

"Who won the pool, Emily?"

"What?"

"You said you had a pool going. Who put money down on us doing so well at slaying your evil asses that you had to turn off key card access?" I asked her. "Anybody win that pool?"

She just blinked those gigantic eyes.

"Why don't you come on down here and undergo the Knife Test yourself, Emily?"

Gregory shouted for me and Ayesha from somewhere on the floor, so I turned away from the alien, no longer interested, and that prompted her to respond.

"Where are you going, Clint?"

"Away from you. Hey, everybody, moon her for me, will ya?"

All the naked humans gathered around the door promptly turned and bent over, presenting their filthy asses to Emily. She probably didn't understand the insult, but it made us all feel better anyway.

We found Gregory standing next to what looked at first like a meat saw, a blood-splattered cutting area underneath a device that hovered over it like a half moon, supported on one end by a jointed adjustable armature.

"What you got?"

He flipped it on and a tight beam of blue-white light lanced down to the cutting surface, stopping a millimeter above it. "This is a laser cutting torch. Overkill if you use it on us, but I imagine it would be necessary for other species with tougher bones than ours, or maybe a dense exoskeleton that a regular meat saw would have trouble with."

"Holy shit."

"I'm pretty sure it's self-contained with its own power source. If we can get it off here it might cut through that door."

"Or any door," I said.

"We wouldn't need key cards," Ayesha mused. "Let's try it. What do you need?"

Gregory pointed to a series of bolts fastening a brace to the table. "Something to loosen those. We need a set of their tools."

Ayesha got everyone on it, as that was our best shot at getting out of there. Teddy found some rolled up in a splattered apron and one of the wrenches worked just fine.

We quickly discovered that the cutter was dense and heavy as fuck and the armature was heavy too since it needed to support all that. Two people needed to hold the half-moon cutter, and another needed to hold on to the armature so it wouldn't flop around and concuss somebody. Gregory searched for a way to disconnect the armature but there weren't any handy bolts at the top; it was manufactured as a single piece, so we asked for a three-person cutting crew to man it and we got it fast, plus a second and third team to tag in once the first one got tired. We were going to rotate shifts and be as efficient and murderous as a group of naked people could be.

The man who'd come to my aid against the slaughterhouse alien found me at that point; he was an actual linebacker for the Buffaloes named Derron Folsom, and he thanked me for leaving him the knife. He'd also been kidnapped from the Rocky Mountain National Park by Emily while hiking with one of his teammates.

"Your teammate wasn't a nose tackle by any chance, was he?"

"Yeah. You know him?"

"Met him very briefly. He charged into the main stairwell full of mishawan and I assume those aliens got got, but I don't know if he's okay or what."

"Oh, man. That makes me feel good. I was worried he'd already…you know," he said, gesturing to the corner of the abattoir where humans were strung up on hooks. "He might be gone now but at least he got to go out fighting. That's all we can ask for at this point."

"Nah, man. We can ask to win."

His eyebrows shot up. "You think?"

"Well, we got a laser now." I hooked a thumb at Ayesha. "And she's got a plan."

THE PLAN

"All right, look," Ayesha said to a group of us gathered around. Everyone in earshot was supposed to relay instructions to those out of earshot. "They gonna know we got a laser if they don't already. They gonna figure out real fast what we wanna do with it. So we have to move faster than they can deal with. We're on Deck Seven. The bridge is on Deck One. Once we get through the door here, everyone get up the stairs as fast as possible. The laser team will come behind, with the tag teams acting as a rear guard. Everyone who's going first, we need you to clear the way and secure any unsecured doors going up. And when you get to Deck One, be ready for anything. Because they won't be playing. We're not playing either. This ain't about saving our asses. This is about saving all the oblivious asses on Earth. All your families and friends. Once we get to the bridge door, we cut through and take over."

"Then what?" Teddy asked.

"Let's get to that point and figure it out from there. Team One, you're up. Cut us out of here."

"Hey, everyone?" I said before we broke up. "I don't know all your names. I hope I get a chance to know you better. But in case I don't get a chance, I just want to say I love you all."

Ayesha cackled. "Damn, Clint. You're all in your feelings. Mushier than mashed potatoes. Which is to say, thank you, and I love y'all too. But right now I need y'all to get the hell out of your loving headspace and have a seat in your murder shop. Let's go."

As one, we grunted and moved toward the door, shifting our headspaces into what Ayesha called our murder shop. Which is, I suppose, a thing that humans can do: shift headspaces, emotional bathrobes, whatever, from one extreme to another. I didn't know if the mishawan could do that or not. I didn't know if they even had a suite of emotions regarding love in all its many variations. Our intercourse to this point had not lent itself to cultural exchange. If I knew that Emily had a journal of love poems stashed somewhere, would that make me hesitate to kill her? Probably not. Whoever she loved would want to eat me just as much as she did. The stakes of mercy were simply too high. And she had a whole lot of payback coming anyway.

The laser cutter was awkward and there was an awful lot of grunting from Team One to get the door sliced open, but they did it and handed the cutter off to Team Two afterward. Derron kicked the cut rectangle out of the center and surprised a group of mishawan on the other side that had their backs to us, pushing down the hallway. There were human bodies—live and paralyzed, so far as we could tell—littering the floor outside the door. And there was an awful lot of noise from more humans trying to get past a row of shielded aliens—probably why they didn't hear us cutting the door. Teddy and I were first through the breach and discovered that this group of aliens not only had the equivalent of police riot shields, but they had weapons also. And they weren't knives.

The use of projectiles and incendiaries are generally no-nos on board spacecraft. The chance of blowing a hole in the hull just isn't worth it and explosive decompression tends to cut short any feeling of victory one might feel at defeating an enemy. Likewise, a bullet in an engine or a life support system can ruin everyone's day. But the mishawan liked their blood toxins and weren't above launching some poisoned razor disks at unprotected humans. They weren't high velocity enough to penetrate the ship's walls or equipment, but they sank into unprotected flesh just fine, a centimeter or two. And while it did take a few seconds to activate, the toxin was one hundred percent effective. The fallen testified to that.

There were six mishawan standing behind shields holding off a mob of naked humans, and six behind them firing poisoned disks into the mob with practically guaranteed hits. As the paralytic shut down their neuromuscular control, they collapsed and became obstacles to others and the mishawan were able to slowly advance over the fallen. Behind the shooters were a pair of others carrying binders for arms and legs, to keep the paralyzed helpless once the venom wore off. That was how they were going to take back control.

We could have just turned right and headed up the stairwell, let them carry on. But one of the aliens trailing behind and putting binders on people looked like a small blonde white girl, wearing a pink ballcap and a unicorn shirt.

It was Janelle.

The one who ate Derek.

JANELLE

I didn't erupt in a battle cry or even say a word to the rest of group emerging from Food Processing. I just charged her, splitting off from the group and suddenly not caring if anything else worked out except avenging my friend. That's all I wanted, and once in range I leapt at her in a flying tackle.

Unfortunately she saw me just before impact and dodged aside, taking only a glancing blow as I skidded past. She was knocked down but unhurt, and her cry of alarm alerted the aliens with guns that they had a problem on their six.

I scrambled to my feet as fast as I could, but it wasn't fast enough to keep Janelle down nor fast enough to avoid the razor disks that shredded through my shirt and tore into my back. I had seconds before my muscles seized up, so I didn't hesitate. I charged Janelle again, extending my shielded arm out as she whipped off her ballcap to set her stingers free.

She attempted to jump over my arm to get to my face but I raised it up and caught her on the shield, propelling her to the wall and trapping her there. There was no time to tell her "this is for Derek" or anything pithy. I just pistoned my right fist as hard as I could into her right eye and it plowed right through to the wall, and then the toxins froze me up with her hooked onto the end of my arm. Her mouth moved, made screeching noises, her stingers plunged too late into my flesh, and she slid down to the floor with me as Teddy and the rest of the escapees charged in to back my play.

They messed up that mishawan riot control good. Coming in from behind them like we did, the ones with guns had to turn and confront the new threat. But that caused them several problems. One, we weren't facing shields so we could overwhelm them eventually. And without them firing into the mob on the other side of the shield wall, that mob could get its own momentum going and press back.

Overwhelming sounds like something that's super easy to do, because the semantics imply you simply get over whatever you need to whelm the shit out of. But it's one thing to say you have overwhelming numbers and another thing to be one of the vanguard that has to meet the enemy first.

My vision was partially obscured by my fall but I caught some of what happened. Teddy had a bucket he was using for a shield, and Derron was coming too with a bucket-and-knife combo. I heard Derron say,

"Goddammit, not again," before he fell next to me. Then I got stepped on a lot as the overwhelming thing happened, the folks in the back coming in to finish off what I started, and that hurt a whole lot more than the stings of the razor disks. But they happily stepped on Janelle too and squashed the hell out of her. I got splattered with blood—both human and mishawan—and someone died on top of me, I think, which meant I saw very little after that.

I moaned in pain even though I knew the bruises from the trampling would heal eventually. What hurt most was the very real possibility that I was out of it now. For better or worse, I'd been removed from the battle and wouldn't get to see the plan carried out. The mishawan riot squad was routed in perhaps thirty or forty seconds of intense fighting, but the battle would flow past me and leave me to shake off the venom eventually, just like all the others on the deck. That is if this venom even wore off at the same rate as the regular dose delivered by their stingers.

Ayesha's voice cut through the din and gave me hope, though. "Where's Clint?" she demanded.

Teddy's voice replied, "Over there, I think."

"Get him. He seems to know a lot of shit and we might need him."

Whatever or whoever was on top of me was soon moved and I was hauled to an awkward sitting position by Teddy. He shucked the remains of Janelle's lifeless body off my arm with a loud slurping noise, then hoisted me up and draped me over his shoulder, much as I had done with Oscar and Gregory. The profound difference was that when I had executed those fireman carries, I had been wearing clothes.

Teddy was not.

Teddy had been in a confined area for days without any sort of sanitation or attention to hygiene, and the nature of the fireman's carry meant that my nose was in close proximity to his ass.

In other circumstances—say, if we were excellent friends and he was wearing jeans—it would have been a fine ass worthy of a casual compliment, and Teddy would walk happily about the world secure in the knowledge that he was providing an excellent rear view. In these circumstances I almost wished Ayesha had forgotten about me and left me in that hallway.

I closed my eyes for the bumpy ride up the stairs. There was nothing to see. There was just plenty of shouting and grunting and time to think of what all the other quantum Clint Beechams might be doing in more pleasant timelines. I didn't even know where I was in the column charging up the stairs. The vanguard again?

Nah. I had to be bringing up the rear.

✳

Teddy Gopal was a kind if odiferous carrier, narrating for me what was happening as we ascended, and I couldn't even be a little bit annoyed with him because I'm sure I would not have smelled any better if I'd been through what he had. At first, he merely acknowledged progress. "Deck Six... Deck Five..."

But once we got to Deck Four we stopped. "There's fighting above us," he explained. "The doors aren't secure. Looks like...yes. Every deck. The aliens are contesting entry. We can't move up with the laser cutter until we get those secure. The people above three are basically trapped. But...yes. We can move up reinforcements to three. I'm going to move aside."

We squished close to the wall on the landing to make room for more people to climb past us and take the fight to Deck Three. The jailbreak meant we had plenty of bodies to throw at the problem, and the mishawan had to be stretched thin. If all was going well, they had two other stairwells to defend from us in addition to this one. Though ours was probably a priority since ours was the one with the laser cutter.

Teddy started encouraging people behind us to squeeze past and get up there to fight. It was a long, tense time, being able to see nothing but his back yet hearing and smelling everything. What I heard was human shouts and grunts mixed with high-pitched mishawan shrieks. People kept climbing past us, heavy footfalls just out of my vision, yet the problem didn't seem to budge.

"There's a pile of bodies on the Deck Three landing," Teddy said. "Bloody mess. Some dead, some paralyzed. Difficult to rush."

Hot pinpricks of pain coursed through me as the toxin broke down and my muscles could feel and respond again.

"Let me down, Teddy," I said.

"Oh! You're back? Fantastic."

There was some grunting from both of us and I was unsteady for a little bit, but I thanked him for his trouble. I still had my shield on my left arm because I'd had my hand and forearm fully inserted into the slit, but I no longer had a weapon.

Teddy was in the opposite situation. He'd held on to his knife but had ditched the bucket.

"What are we dealing with? Just their stingers or those disk guns?"

"The guns, I think."

"We need shields."

"We don't have any."

"We have all we need. The bodies are already there, right? Use people as shields and push out from the door, and then we can just have folks with weapons leap out from behind and take them down."

"Or we build a barricade of bodies that secures the door. We don't have to clear the deck completely. We just need to keep them from interrupting our progress at the door so we can get to Deck One."

I blinked. "Right you are."

Teddy gave the basic idea to a couple of people in passing but they just looked at him oddly and kept going as if he'd asked for loose change. He turned to me in frustration.

"You give the orders because you're wearing clothes. Nobody listens to naked guys."

I laughed because it was probably true. "All right, let's go."

The laser cutters were lining the stairs up to Deck Three and I passed Gregory among them, who was currently holding the device. Someone shouted my name from below, and I turned to see who it was.

"Derron! Get up here." He'd been taken down at the same time I had so it made sense that he'd be up the stairwell as soon as his muscles obeyed him again. And he had his shield and knife. While we had a sliver of everyone's attention, I kept talking. "Everyone listen. You're new and might not know the plan." It took a couple seconds for people to stop, but the fact that I was wearing clothes and claimed to have a plan worked. Teddy was right. "We have a laser cutter that needs to get up to Deck One. But these aliens on Three are a problem. So we need to take the door and hold it and clear a path for the cutters. We're going to do that with bodies. Human shields. You pick one up or you get a volunteer and you use that to just advance and push them back, create all the space you can around that door so the cutter crews can pass. Later on you buy a drink for whoever you used as a shield. We have to work together. Let's go!"

Ayesha, I assumed, was higher up, either on Two or trying to get to One, and I hoped she was okay.

It became clear as we ascended that the mishawan didn't only have the door contested, but the landing itself. At least one of them decided to lean over and pop some poisoned rounds at us on the stairs, and one of them hit Derron in the shoulder.

"God DAMN it!" he said. "I'm going down again! Someone use me as a shield!"

Teddy turned to face me. "Use me, Clint," he said. "Take my knife. I'll help with the weight as long as I can."

I didn't argue. Teddy was a tad leaner than me but otherwise the perfect size for a shield. He threw his arms around my neck and I removed my shield and gave it to someone else before I gripped him by the armpits, but very carefully in the case of the right hand, which was also gripping the knife. I had to sort of smoosh the hilt into the pit so that the blade pointed out from his back. The first couple of steps were really difficult to negotiate with his legs in the way.

"You know what? Just wrap your legs around my waist," I said.

"You sure?"

"I didn't build up these legs with cycling for nothing. Do it."

Coming up the stairs, my legs were a small target anyway and didn't need much protection. Teddy went for it and as soon as he was locked on I charged up as best as I could, which was a sort of a lumbering charge as hauling a full-grown man up the steps is a tough ask, even when you've got some tree trunks for thighs. They saw us coming and Teddy hissed as a couple of razor disks sank into his back.

"Ohh, I hate them so much," he said. "I'm gonna be out in a sec. Good hunting, Clint. Ugh!"

Two more hit him and he fell silent, but his bulk was doing the job of protecting me. One of the mishawan on the landing aimed a kick at us but I saw that shit coming and twisted a bit so that the knife took him on the bottom of the foot. He retracted that quickly and screamed and I barreled him over with Teddy serving as a ram. I stomped down hard on his head and it popped, blue goo sliming my heel, even as I pivoted to block incoming rounds from two more mishawan—one on the landing near the door and one standing directly in the doorway. There were more behind that one on Deck Three, and that's where we needed to push out. But damn if there wasn't just a mess of bodies on the landing, both human and alien, making footing uncertain. The alien whose head I'd stomped was twitching, and Teddy wasn't getting any lighter. My breaths were already coming fast and hard. I shuffled to my right and lunged at the nearest mishawan, the awkwardly clasped knife pointed at his face, and he helpfully gave ground and backed into the doorway, much to the shrieking dismay of his companions. I realized that if I pushed through that door they'd be able to flank me on either side of it, and that would quickly end Clint and Ted's excellent adventure. We needed to push through at some point, however, because we wouldn't be able to close the door otherwise. The doors opened into the stairwell— presumably to make sure the corridors maintained a certain clearance—so in theory I could close it without going through the door first, but the mishawan would not let me do that.

Teddy's legs had slipped from around my waist and now I was holding his weight entirely in my hands underneath his armpits. It was suboptimal, but it was thwarting the mishawan for the moment.

"A little help?" I cried, and I got it. Two more teams who had copied our idea charged up, but since the person acting as a shield hadn't taken a hit yet, they were helping to bear the weight. They told me to clear out of the way and I stepped aside as they plowed their way through the door, taking the brunt of the mishawan fury but also clearing out space enough for a horde of single fighters to swarm through and overwhelm their position. I gave someone my knife and then hollered that we needed to clear the landing of bodies and secure the door. As that unfolded—the mishawan bodies were just tossed down the open middle of the stairwell to fall all the way to Deck Ten—I moved Teddy into the corner of the landing and turned him around to face it.

"I'm going to pull these razors out and hopefully we'll get a chance to tape them up soon."

There were five all told—somehow I'd missed one of the impacts. They bled but they weren't shooting out arterial sprays, so he'd heal up all right.

"That was good," I told him. "That worked. We got this door now. Can you make any noise at all, like a vowel sound?"

"Eeeee," Teddy said.

"Good. Let's do eeeee for yes, ooooo for no." I hated using Emily's system, but it was practical. "Okay, you have five doses of mishawan juice in you and we don't know how long it will take to wear off. Do you want to go with me or sit it out? Yes for go with me, no for sit it out."

"Eeeee."

"Okay, up it is." I waved to people to get moving. "Secure Decks Two and One!"

Some more folks charged up to Deck Two, which succumbed fairly quickly with a new supply of bodies to throw at it, and then we closed the doors to both landings so that the laser cutting crew could ascend. I hoisted Teddy over my shoulder and climbed up to the stairs leading to Deck One and led the crew. It was exhausting and I was breathing pretty hard, but I preferred this scenario to being carried by Teddy. Ayesha was on the top landing with a couple of others, one man attempting to twist the handle to no avail.

"Hey, Clint. They've got us locked out here."

"A quick shot with the cutter right above the handle will make them let go and then you can open it and charge through."

"I like the way you think. Let's do it."

I had to get out of the way and wait on the steps so that Gregory and his cutter crew could deploy the laser on the door. Ayesha made sure she had a team in place with knives and makeshift shields and then the crew did their thing. An alien scream on the other side let us know that the laser had burned one of them. A man I didn't know tried the handle and it opened easily. He swung open the door and Ayesha leapt forward with two others to meet only three mishawan on the other side, one of them wounded. Ayesha got tagged with stingers despite her shield and went down, paralyzed, and so did the others first through the door, but our follow-ups swarmed them and busted their heads.

That left me temporarily in charge, because Gregory looked to me and said, "Now what, Clint?" I wasn't sure if having Teddy's ass in close proximity to my face gave me more or less authority, but apparently I had enough to issue orders.

"We get to the bridge. I don't know why that door was so poorly guarded. They had to know we were coming."

Gregory pointed down the corridor where a small cluster of naked people suddenly appeared around a corner.

"I think at least one of the other stairwells made it to the top as well."

I'd somehow forgotten about everyone else, but remembered that we should have a huge advantage in numbers if all the prisoners had been released.

"Good. The plan's worked so far. They weren't prepared to deal with a jailbreak like that." The mishawan were more than able to take us in small numbers, but literal thousands of desperate humans were not going to be handled by anything short of a large riot suppression team—and they'd sent a small one down to our end. But that didn't mean other teams hadn't found more success. Once I realized that we should actually be seeing more humans up here, not so few, it hinted that the mishawan were having success in containing us somewhere below.

"Can someone carry Ayesha? Let's get to the bridge."

CAPTAIN EMILY

"Hi, Clint!" Emily's face appeared on a door monitor screen as we passed it but I didn't slow down.

"Keep going," I said to everyone, and we marched on.

"Clint?" She showed up on another door and I ignored that one too. She tried to stop me at the next one with a threat. "Clint, I can still tell my people on Earth to wipe out your family."

I didn't even break stride, and didn't bother to speak directly at the camera, but rather assumed she'd be able to hear me. "Doesn't matter what you do. You're dying today."

"There is no way we will let you take the bridge. We'll scuttle the ship."

"That's absolutely fine with us," I said, and it was. "You do that." In another timeline Letitia and I were happy and living our best lives. Buying cheeses we couldn't pronounce, a spa day once a year, shit like that. Here I'd had it good and fine for at least a little while, and considering how badly things could have gone for me long before this, I was coming around to the idea that I could exit any time with no regrets. I'd gotten Janelle, at least, and that was something.

"Our goal is to make sure you never get home, Emily. So go ahead. Fuck us all up right now. Humanity wins. Pretty sure nobody picked that one in your pool."

Emily appeared on another monitor as I kept walking, her joviality all gone. "This isn't over, Clint."

"Oh, I know. Not yet. But it will be soon, one way or another."

Next monitor: "If you try that cutter on the bridge door, Clint, you won't like what's waiting on the other side."

"Is that supposed to make me give up? I already don't like what's on the other side."

She didn't bother me after that. We turned a corner and came athwart a crowded corridor of naked escapees, at the end of which was a sealed door that humans were pounding on.

"Make way, please!" I shouted. "We have a laser cutter." I had to repeat myself multiple times, but eventually the crowd parted and let us pass.

Gregory wasn't actually on the crew hauling the cutter at the moment—it was Team Three, I believe, that was schlepping it around at this point, because it was still heavy as fuck, but the old robotics expert enjoyed the cheering that ensued when people realized what this meant.

When we got to the door, I turned and faced everyone and held up my hands for silence. Once everyone was listening—and I assumed the mishawan were too—I said, "Hey everyone. I'm Clint. This ass here on my shoulder belongs to RAF Lieutenant Teddy Gopal, and he's a great guy but a bit paralyzed at the moment. He'll talk to you later."

Some polite laughter. "There's going to be one hell of a fight on the other side of this door. Chances of negotiating a deal where they just take us home and forget about us are zero. It's much more likely they'll scuttle the ship to keep us from taking control. But getting home is not the point for us now, is it? We just need to make sure *they* never get home, and then our home will be safe. Just wanted to be clear on what's at stake and what's about to happen. There's no happy ending for us. There's just a grim one, but we want to make sure theirs is just as grim. So put your murder hats on. When we cut a hole in this door, get in there and kill them all."

A chorus of grunts agreed, and the crew moved toward the door.

"Hold on a second. What are your names?" I asked them.

"Jorge," the one on the left holding the armature said. He was a Latinx man with broad shoulders. "Grant," the ginger white guy in the middle said.

He had a purple birthmark on his right shoulder. "DongWon," said the Korean fellow on the right.

"You guys all get picked up in the same place?"

"Jorge and I are from San Francisco," DongWon affirmed. "They got us in Muir Woods."

"I'm from England," Grant said.

"All right. Jorge, Grant, DongWon, thank you for doing this. I'm glad you're here and we all love you."

They looked at me strangely for a moment but then smiled when they realized I meant it and the nodding heads gathered around did too.

"Thanks," Grant said. They lifted the cutter up to the top of the door and turned it on. They moved it maybe three inches before a percussive whump was heard and then Grant's torso exploded in a spray of blood, shattered bone, and viscera. He dropped dead, and that startled Jorge and DongWon so much that they dropped the cutter entirely with a heavy clunk and it turned off.

The mishawan had projectile weapons after all, and whatever it was traveled clean through the door, Grant's midsection, and came to rest in the torso of another human, a woman standing behind him who cried out and fell next to me, a bullet of some kind in her belly. That did put a damper on our celebratory door-shredding ceremony.

The wounded woman was pulled away and a couple of people were tasked to take her down to the medical deck to see if anything could be done; we needed to know what facilities existed there anyway.

"So I guess we can't cut it open," I said.

"We can. We absolutely can," Gregory said, and then he swallowed audibly before continuing at a louder volume. "That was an officer's weapon. They don't give those to everyone. It's a sidearm, usually ceremonial, but always functional in case you have to put down a deserter or a mutinous cretin. I don't know how many rounds mishawan sidearms can fire without reloading, but it's not infinite. They certainly don't have more rounds than we have people to cut down this door. It's just a matter of who's willing to die now to get it open for the rest of us."

Gregory looked down at the ginger fellow, who lay sprawled on the deck in front of the door with a large portion of his torso missing, and pointed.

"I talked to Grant a bit before," he announced. "He was a butcher from Sheffield. He was taken, like me, from the Peak District National Park in England. He didn't die for Queen and country, and certainly not for the Tory twat at 10 Downing Street, but for all of us. Met him down in the abattoir on Deck Seven. On our way up here, he says to me, 'Y'know how everyone always says you never want to see how the sausage gets made? Truth is we see it every day, one way or another. We're all just meat for the grinder, marinating in this or that until it's our turn to get shoved into the blades.' He might have been right about that. I think he was. You almost never get to choose your time, though, do you? Well: I choose now." He pointed a furious finger at the door. "I'm gonna pick up that cutter and I'm gonna dive face first into the grinder, and when I'm down I expect one of you to take my place and keep going until they're out of bullets and we are through that door and every last one of them is dead. They're gonna blow up the ship and make sausage of us anyway, so we might as well teach them to fear us before they die." He got a rousing cheer of approval for that, and he looked around and caught my eye. "Clint. Ayesha, I know you can hear me. It's been an honor."

I nodded to him. "Likewise. I love you, man."

"And I you."

We cleared out the middle of the corridor and pressed against the sides, and I put Teddy down. The person who'd been carrying Ayesha likewise set her down across from me.

Gregory picked up the laser cutter in concert with Jorge and DongWon and said, "Don't drop it this time. Someone will fill my spot." They assured him they wouldn't drop it and he said, "All right, Emily. Fuuuuuck youuuu."

They turned on the cutter at the top of the door where the previous cut had ended, and in less than two seconds a round obliterated Gregory's head and kept going down the corridor. He fell backward, dead before he hit the deck, but the cutting crew kept the laser going and only wobbled a little bit. I gasped, as did many others, but it hardened our resolve. A woman stepped forward, tears in her eyes, said her name was Yolanda Cisneros, and stretched up her arms to stabilize the cutter. She was shortly blown away in turn. And so the grinding began, and progressed. Sean FitzGibbon was next. Then Leroy Jenkins. Marta Rodriguez, LaToya Washington, Gurpreet Singh, Alan O'Bryan, Madeleine Sturges, and Luc Giroux followed. We who were on the edges dragged the bodies out of the middle, and I would have stepped up myself except that I didn't want to make it that easy for Emily to mow me down. She might get me later anyway, but I wanted to have a chance at giving as good as I got.

Jerry MacInnes from Australia was the twelfth man. Twelve people stood up and got shot down, and we were all angry crying after Gregory. The thirteenth person to stand, Amie Kaufmann, remained standing, and the door to the bridge got cut, but far too slowly to prevent the aliens from scuttling the ship. The order had no doubt been given sometime after they ran out of bullets and before we could bust through. But damn, were we ready to bust through.

Ayesha got her venom broken down before it was done and shouted, "Try not to damage the hardware! Maybe we can do something if it all still works."

Teddy was still paralyzed since he had more toxin to break down, but I assured him I'd come back for him if I could. "And if I don't come back, well, thanks for getting me here."

I had no shield and no weapon, but when that door got kicked down, I didn't hesitate. Ayesha was right behind me and said, "Let's find Emily."

"Hell yes."

"Tackle and smash, people!" Ayesha called. "First person tackle them, second one smash their heads!"

We didn't get any time to look around at the bridge once we got through the door, because it was a churn of bodies and flailing limbs. There were too many in front of us to spot Emily—she wasn't very tall, so I imagined she was waiting behind the wall of flesh somewhere.

The tackle-and-smash tactic was effective only because we outnumbered them four to one or more. There were perhaps a dozen mishawan on the bridge waiting for us, organized and lined up, and they batted aside the first attempts to take them down with their superior strength. But a flying leap from Jorge had enough momentum behind it to take one down and poke a hole in their line, and then more flying leaps followed. The man in front of me looked over his shoulder and said, "Follow up," and then he launched himself at a mishawan holding down their left flank. They went down in a howling tangle and the alien's stingers whipped at the man's face, but a judicious stomp of my foot ended that threat in short order.

And then a small figure plowed into my ribs and knocked me over into a clear space, away from the main action. I knocked the back of my skull on the deck and stars popped off in my vision.

"Hi, Clint!" Emily said, her evil grin leering at me before punching me hard in the teeth with a tiny fist and then leaning down, pinning my much bigger arms with her inhuman strength. "You're too late. We've given the order to scuttle and soon we'll all be atomized. But you saw that coming, didn't you?"

"Yeah," I admitted through a mouthful of teeth. I spat a tooth at her eye and she reared back instinctively, blinking and laughing at my weak response. I said, "Did you see the team we sent back to the engines to prevent that very thing from happening?"

Her grin disappeared. "What team?"

I spat another tooth and it got her pretty good, which I'd been hoping for. She flinched and eased up the pressure on my arms, allowing me to grab her head on both sides and press my thumbs deep into her eyes.

"Here's a probe, silly!" I ground out, blood spraying from between my lips.

Emily screamed and her stingers instinctively lanced into my hands before she grasped my wrists and tore my hands away, but the damage had been done.

"Nope, guess you didn't see them." She didn't see Ayesha coming up behind her either. The biologist swung her right leg around and kicked Emily on the side of her head, knocking her off me but right next to my arm. I raised it up and brought my elbow down on her temple, but managed only to dent it weakly as Emily's venom shut down my muscles. Still, that got her limbs shuddering and she wasn't spouting off cheery death threats anymore.

"Freezing up," I told Ayesha, who hadn't stopped moving. Her focus was entirely on Emily. She brought her right leg up again and whipped the heel down hard onto the very spot where I'd made a dent with my elbow, popping Emily's head in a splatter of blue blood and goo. The body kept twitching and Ayesha jumped up and down on it until it stopped.

"God *damn* but that felt good," she said, grinning. "All right, even if we're all about to explode, I can die happy now."

"Me too," I managed, surprised I could still speak. Ayesha was caught off guard as well, and she turned to me with her eyebrows raised.

"Why aren't you paralyzed yet?"

"I don't know. I mean, I am, partially. Maybe she didn't give me a full dose. Maybe it just hasn't worked its way up to my head yet. Or maybe I'm developing a resistance to it."

"Vive la résistance."

WHAT HAPPENED TO OSCAR

By the time Ayesha got the bridge secured and cleared out, with the mishawan bodies removed and the paralyzed left to break down the venom in the corridor, I had recovered enough to stand again and Teddy had also recovered and joined us. If we weren't doomed as Emily claimed, it would take us a few days to decelerate, accelerate again in the other direction for a while, then decelerate again and take some dick ships down to the Earth's surface, where I would point like hell at the craft to make sure the police knew I really had been kidnapped by aliens and had nothing to do with Derek's murder. With any luck, Emily hadn't been lying and there was food and water enough on the ship for us to make it back. But that was all assuming we knew what we were doing, and we didn't. I had no idea how to pilot this thing. Aside from the maps Emily had given us, everything was labeled in the mishawan language. We were looking at a bunch of buttons and levers that might do the thing we wanted or might jettison something vital.

The monitor and gridded speaker was recognizable, though, that Emily had used to talk to me throughout the ship. Presumably it had a built-in camera and microphone. The buttons arranged around it would address the ship somehow and probably not do anything life-threatening. I pressed some until I appeared on screen and cleared my throat. "Is this thing on? Yeah?" I heard my own voice echo back to me. "Hey everybody, it's Clint Beecham talking to you from the bridge. We've taken over. If you're systematically searching every inch of the ship to make sure every last alien is dead, you should definitely keep doing that. We need Decks Nine and Ten cleared for sure. And Oscar, Hanh, and Deepali, if you can hear me, we'd love to hear from you if you can get us a status update somehow."

We really needed to know if the engines were safe, but I spent some time making sure everyone had a basic knowledge of the ship layout since many of them had no idea. "If you're able to confirm any deck is clear, please have someone come up to the bridge and report it to us until we can figure out ship coms more efficiently."

I signed off for a minute to let reports come in, and to do some math for Ayesha on when we might be able to get home. Teddy was making educated guesses about what certain instruments did based on his general piloting knowledge, but so far he hadn't touched anything because he knew even better than we did what the consequences could be of making a mistake.

"We really need a nice Mishawan to English dictionary," he said.

Reports began to trickle in: Decks One and Two were clear, as well as Four through Six. Three was taking time as that was the crew quarters and they needed to search a lot of little cabins; there were also two more mishawan riot teams on seven and eight that needed to be taken out. As I'd feared, they had effectively neutralized the advance on the forward stairs and were in danger of flanking the middle.

The monitor on the bridge lit up without our prompting and Oscar squinted into it. "Hey. You guys hear me? I see some lights on here, but I don't know if it's working."

"Yes, yes, it's working," Ayesha said, suddenly standing in front of it.

"Oh, hey, Ayesha. Engines secure. We pounced on a group of them trying to do something manually to the housings. Deepali and Hanh are both hurt, and we lost some guys who came with us, but at least the shit's not gonna blow."

"Do you know what kind of engines they are?" I asked. "Or what fuel they're using?"

Oscar shrugged. "Rocket engines, man. I dunno. Space fuel. If you wanted me to list some fancy radioactive isotope, that is not my bag. Like, I don't even know where the fuel gauge is or if we're running low, much less how to refuel when we need it."

I stepped away, disappointed. I'd have to get down there myself to check things out. Ayesha said, "Oscar, do me a favor and just look through the whole area again. We need to be double sure it's secure. Then I guess we'll need to station somebody back there."

"Okay. I'll report back later."

Ayesha found a security station that streamed a feed of the holding areas on Deck Eight, now empty except for one that had been sparsely repopulated by one of the mishawan riot teams. "How do I make this switch to a different view?" she wondered aloud.

"Wait. Hold on. That's a number key."

"What now?"

"We know that's Deck Eight. So one of these symbols on the screen here is the number eight. Let's figure it out."

"Yeah, but how do I do anything?"

"Touch the screen. When they probed me, they had tablets and used touch screens."

Ayesha pressed the screen with her index finger and the pictures changed, as well as the labeling. "Yes!"

"Yes indeed. The first symbols remained the same so we can guess that those mean *Deck*. The last symbol changed so that's the number."

We got our numbers translated that way, at least, and discovered that there were some mishawan stragglers skulking around the freezers on Deck Nine. We dispatched some folks to take care of that and directed others to surround and rush the riot teams so that the ship would truly be ours. There had been a few hundred aliens and they were prepared to take on six of us, but the Reserves had made sure they faced tens of thousands.

It took a half hour for reports of cleared decks to arrive, and then the ship was being systematically searched to free anyone who'd been caught by riot teams and placed in binders.

"All right, Clint, tell everybody the good news," Ayesha said, and we shared a smile, one of those relieved smiles that signal there's hope welling inside of us once again after it had gone dry for a while.

There was a timeline where none of this happened and Derek and I were both in Colorado, loving our spouses and waiting for our children to be born. But as Emily said to me as Derek was being eaten, there was no going back, only forward. There was no doubt a number of timelines where our rebellion failed and the mishawan successfully colonized us. There were also timelines where Gregory survived and I didn't. But this was at least one where the humans prevented the mishawan home world from finding out that Earth existed. If nothing else, that made this one less horrible than others. And if I was really, really lucky, this was also a timeline where I got to go home. That would be my best possible future now. Physics, I have found, can be simultaneously uncompromising and a source of infinite hope, just as the universes it governs are infinite.

"Clint here again," I said over the public address. "I just want to say right now I love you all. You're beautiful people."

"Damn, Clint, you just bust out with those feelings every chance you get," Ayesha said off camera, but I ignored her and continued.

"Out of curiosity, do we have any astronauts or astronomers on board? Or any pilots, mechanical engineers, or maybe a linguist? The ship is now officially ours and Earth is safe, so fuck yeah, go humans! But if we're ever going to get home, well…there's a question of navigation."